I'D LIKE TO SAY SORRY,
BUT THERE'S NO ONE
TO SAY SORRY TO

I'D LIKE TO SAY SORRY,
BUT THERE'S NO ONE
TO SAY SORRY TO

Stories

MIKOŁAJ GRYNBERG

Translated from the Polish by Sean Gasper Bye

THE
NEW
PRESS

NEW YORK
LONDON

This publication has been supported by the ©POLAND Translation Program

© 2017 by Mikołaj Grynberg
English language translation © 2021 by Sean Gasper Bye
All rights reserved.
No part of this book may be reproduced, in any form,
without written permission from the publisher.

Requests for permission to reproduce selections from this book should
be made through our website: https://thenewpress.com/contact.

The stories "Unnecessary Trouble," "Arkadia," "Cacophony," "An Elegant
Purse," "Bitter Chocolate," "My Five Jews," and "An Empty Jewish Soul"
were published, in slightly different form, in *Jewish Currents* in 2019.

Originally published in Poland as *Rejwach* by Wydawnictwo Nisza, 2017
Published in the United States by The New Press, New York, 2021
Distributed by Two Rivers Distribution

ISBN 978-1-62097-683-8 (hc)
ISBN 978-1-62097-685-2 (ebook)
CIP data is available

The New Press publishes books that promote and enrich public discussion
and understanding of the issues vital to our democracy and to a more
equitable world. These books are made possible by the enthusiasm of
our readers; the support of a committed group of donors, large and
small; the collaboration of our many partners in the independent
media and the not-for-profit sector; booksellers, who often hand-
sell New Press books; librarians; and above all by our authors.

www.thenewpress.com

Composition by dix!
This book was set in Centaur MT

Printed in the United States of America

2 4 6 8 10 9 7 5 3 1

My thanks
go first and foremost to Jakub Bierzyński,
who at a crucial moment created the conditions
for me to be able to write this book.
If not for Junona Lamcha-Grynberg, Justyna Dąbrowska,
Paweł Łoziński, Paweł Malko, Marcin Grynberg, Karina
Sokołowska, Patrycja Dołowy, Barbara Engelking, and Paweł Żak
I would not have known whether the stories I have to tell
would interest anyone other than myself.
The amount of strength you've given me allows me
to risk confronting my readers.
To my children, Aleks and Tosia, for reading some of these
stories and, right afterwards, letting me see them through your eyes.

Contents

CONTENTS

I'D LIKE TO SAY SORRY,
BUT THERE'S NO ONE
TO SAY SORRY TO

Unnecessary Trouble

I was properly scared to meet you in my town. What's to say no one would recognize you? Better to keep our heads down than have somebody see us both there. Maybe somebody's read one of those Jewish books of yours. That kind of trouble I don't need one bit. I thought to myself, I'll get on a train, a couple of hours and I'm there, and I'm sure it's more comfortable for you to meet locally than ride a couple of hours like that. It's good you agreed; I was worried you'd insist on coming with some documents or photos to look at. We'd have had to hide for sure. Just like those people in your books. I'd have been ashamed and that would have been the end of it, because how would that look—inviting a Jew to come hide.

If you want to ask me some questions, go ahead, but I'll warn you I've got everything thought through already. Well, maybe not everything, but plenty. First of all, how are you going to make sure no one works out it's me? Because I'd rather leave out my town, my name, my age, my job, and definitely how I look. Because, I mean, that's the easiest way to recognize a person. That's probably enough, right? I think it's enough, and you've got to promise that's exactly what you'll do. I'm sorry to be so blunt right off the bat, but you know how it is. The kind of trouble you write about in those books of yours, I don't need that one bit.

Speaking of which, all that stuff is more than a normal person can imagine. You made up a few of those stories there, right? About half of them have got to be made up, which means the rest are true, right? Fine, it's no business of mine anyhow; even without you I've got enough trouble of my own.

Will you tell me what it is about you, you Jews, that whatever anyone says about you, it's never a neutral subject? I'm talking so much because I've got a story to tell you but I somehow can't get started. I'd planned out just about everything on the train, but in person like this it feels totally different. Listen, what is it with you guys that you make everything so complicated? With me, things are simple, because I work where I told you, I'm as old as I said was, I've already described my family, and there you go, everything's clear. But not with you guys! First you've got to deceive everybody, then frighten everybody, then shock them, and then at the very end you die and leave a great big mess. You get what I'm saying? Maybe I'm talking all jumbled—I don't want to say talking like a Jew—I'm working up to it, but I'm doing the best I can.

Luckily, I bought a two-way ticket, so I wouldn't have too much time with you. That's why I keep looking at my watch, not out of bad manners. Has anybody else wanted to tell you a story or am I the only one? Well, what does it matter to me anyhow. All right, now or never! I have a lot of questions, a lot of resentment, but you're the least guilty of anyone in all this. It's not your fault my sister showed me your books. But the subject had already come up by then! Only that's not your fault either.

Will you tell me if it works for you guys like in the jokes about Jews, how when a Jewish man dies, he summons his whole family and they stand around him, and he pronounces these words of wisdom and says something special to everyone? Because if it is, I don't know why you joke about it! Does death amuse you? Death isn't funny to me, especially when someone close to you dies. Someone where you've known her since you were born and know everything about her, because her whole life she told every one of us her stories a hundred times each. And then you find out you know a little bit, but mostly you don't.

Our grandmother died, almost a year ago now. But before she did, she managed to tell us what you're probably already imagining. We're standing beside that bed of hers, the whole family. Parents, me and my sister and our little kids, and suddenly, before you know it, she's saying she's a Jew and she couldn't pass away without telling us. We look at one another and can't believe our ears, because we're not big fans of the Jews.

3

My sister takes me off to the side and says Grandma's not getting enough oxygen now, that's why she's talking like that. But Grandma doesn't give up. She starts telling our family story. About those ghettos of yours, those camps, Auschwitzes, sisters, brothers, gas, and all the rest. What's a normal person supposed to make of all that? And I'm telling you, it wasn't like in a Jewish joke.

The next day our grandmother, a non-Jew her entire life, died. And who was left? Her Jewish daughter and her Jewish grandkids, right? Because that's how it works with you guys, right? And what are we expected to do? We're not even sure anybody knows about this except us and you. It wasn't a message she passed on to us, it was fear. I came here on behalf of my family to thank you for that fear. Who was I supposed to go to, the parish priest? Your stories, you deal with them yourself. I'm going, or else I'll miss my train.

Arkadia

You know how fall gets here. Rain or shine, the dog's got to go out. I run into various unfortunates from around the world, wandering baffled through my neighborhood. They have distinguishing marks: a map of Warsaw in one hand, a map of the ghetto printed off the internet in the other. They come all year round, but fall is when I feel most sorry for them. They're looking this way and that; you can tell from a distance they're helpless as babies. And I stand there with my dog and think to myself: to help or not to help? Sometimes I go up to them, though my English is so terrible I don't really talk to them. I just give a friendly smile and say, in my heavy accent, *"Ken I help yoo?"* They mainly ask for *"Mee-la bun-ker"* and *"Ra-pa-port,"* though recently I've also gotten *"myoo-zee-um."* The Jewish museum is easy, the Jewish partisans' bunker on Miła Street I also got quickly; it took me a while to work out "Rapaport" referred to the sculptor of the Ghetto Heroes memorial.

Most of them are really suspicious. I get why they don't

trust a random Polish man, but it's hard to reach out to someone who's being so prickly. *"Mee-la bun-ker,"* all right—let's go. I live nearer to John Paul II Avenue, so it's about six hundred meters to the bunker on Miła Street. The conversation doesn't flow, because I look like an adult, but one who doesn't know how to talk. I do my best, I smile. . . . I stay a little off to one side, a little ahead, so they feel safe. And I wonder what stories their parents or grandparents told them about us Poles. They talk amongst themselves in various languages, usually Hebrew or English.

Normally I take a straight path to the bunker, but if there are any excavations going on, I change my route, I avoid them, because I'm afraid of what people might see there. This I learned with some young people, from Israel, I think. We're walking, smiling warmly, gorgeous weather because it's summer, then they stop all of a sudden and peer into this pit. I'm standing a little further off, but even from there I know what they've seen. They turn to me and ask, *"Hyoo-man bonz?"* And I mean, what am I supposed to tell them? I nod sadly. They've worked it out anyway, they're only looking for confirmation. They're standing there, the two of them, tears flowing down their cheeks, and I don't know what to do with myself. If I knew how, I'd work up the courage to say I cry over those bones too. I'd give them a hug, and maybe they'd even return the embrace.

✳

I prefer older tourists, they're nicer, more open. I talk to them more as we walk those six hundred meters. A lot of the time young people treat me like I'm trying to get money out of them. I swallow these silent insults. I know by the corner of Miła and Dubois they'll want to get rid of me, but a few try to pay me. I can cope with that. The worst is when they're thanking me and they say, "*Yu ar a gud Pol.*" I can't even explain how much that hurts me. If they knew that for years I've been collecting all the bones sticking out of the ground and looking for a fitting place for them, then maybe they'd say I'm a "*veri gud Pol.*"

I used to inform the city; I would ask them to make sure the bones got buried. Then I would call around to various Jewish organizations. I was looking for a contact to the Jewish Community. But I realized that for religious reasons the rabbis would fight to halt the construction and I got scared of how the locals would react. Now I don't call anyone. I come at night and gather up the bones in plastic bags. At first, I used to take them to the Jewish cemetery and quietly bury them right beside the wall. But someone might have thought I was digging something up, rather than burying it. Recently, I've found a perfect place for them. I hope their souls will finally find eternal rest there.

I bury them at night on a slope by the Arkadia mall. I walk home with my dog, believing I've done good.

Cacophony

Something gives me the sense these days that being a Jew is harder than not being a Jew. I've got a little age and experience; I'm happy to tell you what all this cacophony is about.

You're born and you don't know who you are. If you're born into a better home you've got it better, into a worse one, it's worse. For your parents, the early days are the most enjoyable. You get what I'm saying? The very, absolute beginnings of bringing a person into the world are well worth recommending. These two people go on walks together, hold hands, climb into bed, and then they wake up, and a new person is ready to go. They might have planned ahead, found a way around it, but at that moment, you see, they're not thinking. The only thing on their minds is to climb into bed. They're not thinking about anything, not even how the world will be enriched by you, which is to say by me, because I don't know much about you, but nowadays I know a heck of a lot about myself.

A little time goes by and this person is born, just like in an obstetrics handbook. Here we do it lying down, other places they do it squatting. It's not worth talking about, because the instant this little boy takes a whiff of our rust-colored air he's done for. He's got to live here till he dies. Whether he grows up to be a brainiac or a schmuck, he's got to live and there's nothing he can do about it.

When a person like that, let's say little Miron, is born to Izaak and Nehuma, it's not the same as if he'd been born to Stanisław and Jadwiga. And now just you think how complicated it gets to be born in a country that's made more for Stanisław and Jadwiga than for Izaak and Nehuma. Those first two think it's theirs and they're not the only ones who think that, so the second two, even though they've lived here for eight generations or more, don't argue.

Their little Miron grows up and wants to study, but now it turns out Stanisław, Jadwiga, and a couple of other folks don't want him to go to college, and those schools he dreamed of slam the door in his face. And so Miron has become a Jew.

But he doesn't go to Palestine to make the desert bloom, even though some of Izaak and Nehuma's relatives are planning to. He doesn't go to yeshiva to pick apart abstract dilemmas either. He wants to become a doctor. He goes to whatever school accepts his application.

Years later, Miron is a physician first and foremost. To

some he's a doctor, to others, a Jewish doctor. Compared to what he's got coming, let me tell you, this is a walk in the park.

And now comes a time that will make Miron a Jew through and through. He has to leave his own home, and wear a Star of David to put a seal on his Jewishness—he finds himself in bondage. Not Egyptian bondage—the world's moved on after all—but a bondage that's meant to resolve the Jewish question in the blink of an eye.

He'd prefer not being a Jew, because staying alive is better than being sentenced to extermination. Sadly, he's not the one writing the rules of the game and finally he loses. But this story has moments worth recommending, just like with Izaak and Nehuma. Miron managed to climb into bed with a certain Sara and, utterly unnecessarily, they made a person.

This new person is in a tough spot but he's been given a chance: a name out of the same catalog as Stanisław and Jadwiga's. He's become Jurek. He'll be able to go to college. From time to time, he thinks back to the dark basements and not being allowed to make the slightest noise. Luckily the memories pass, leaving room for life. Every Jurek is the master of his life. So some people think.

History has been letting him breathe a little, but it's not long before it shows its familiar face. It's 1968 and Jurek has become Jewish through and through. Until now his Jewishness was only for his own purposes, but from now on others will use it for theirs as well. Jurek, like each of his ancestors, learns he's not at home. He always felt this was home, he had friends and places here he couldn't imagine his life without. But Jewish fate has caught up with Jurek. Our Jurek was foolish and naïve, but now he's got to quickly come down to earth. He weighs the greater and lesser evil, though he'd rather have the option of at least one good good. He's waging a Jewish war. In a Jewish war, a Jew fights his own thoughts and always loses. Jurek doesn't set off on a journey, as centuries-long tradition dictates; he stays with his mom. But his mom does what moms do—after a few years, she dies.

Now Jurek knows he's inherited being a Jew. His life is no better or worse than other Jewish lives. Any of those lives might also have forced him to consider setting off on a pretty serious journey. Of course, you lose things on the way, but hear me out, the man who loses nothing is lost. And that sort of lifeless life is only for those who're partial to life after death. I am not one of them. As far as I can tell, Jurek isn't either.

And now I'll start over and give you some advice: I think it's better not to be a Jew, because, you see for yourself, folks aren't exactly lining up for the privilege. It's too late for you now, but you might still take some girl or another by the hand, go on a walk, and then climb into bed with that girl or a different one, maybe even both, climb into bed for a moment.

You climb into bed, you get up, you wait and keep your mouth shut! Don't tell that new person anything! Get out of here before other people tell him. That's how you save Jews.

I didn't promise it would be pleasant.

You can still climb into bed and get a positive result; me, all I can do is climb into bed and wait for the final one.

An Elegant Purse

I used to keep leaving, now I can't stop coming back.

I thought everyone fought with their mother, so I didn't worry about it too much. We fought ferociously and in silence, mother and daughter. There were no explosions, just the sort of hiss of a lit fuse. Obviously, a hiss leads to an explosion and it's something to be afraid of. How many times could it hiss without exploding? I figured Mom could hiss without me, so I ran away to the edge of Europe. I'd finished my first year of studying something or other, which I wasn't enjoying anyway. Leaving was the christening of my adulthood. I was working, paying for a room, cultivating dreadlocks and also a notebook full of resentments toward the entire world.

A year later, I returned for the funeral of a distant cousin on my father's side. I didn't stick around long. I made it back to the edge of Europe before that familiar hiss had the chance to start up again. All in all, I could count that as a successful trip.

In a new place, I started studying something much more

interesting, and I traded my room for a student apartment. I grew my dreads out and kept writing to my mom. I could feel how important we were to one another, but putting it down on paper kept us safe from nonexplosions.

I went back for the second time a few years later, unexpectedly. Dad got sick. I dropped out of my last semester of college. While we were burying Dad, I asked if we could go visit Mom's family grave. I'd never been there but I knew it existed because I'd heard her mention it to Dad. We didn't go. Mom was hissing again.

I went back home. Now I had my own life, a boyfriend, a shared apartment, and a new citizenship. I stopped writing to Mom. We kept email and Skype on hand in case of anything unanticipated. I graduated, got married, had a daughter. I cut off my dreads and moved into my own apartment. I wrote to Mom that I was an adult and I wanted to be treated like one. Mom wrote back three weeks later saying she'd pay for me to come visit. I left my daughter with my husband and I went. We'd both missed each other a lot.

I demanded we go together to Mom's family grave. Mom stopped talking to me. I didn't set eyes on the grave. I changed my ticket and went back to my family early.

It took another few years for Mom to make up her mind to get in touch. I'd really been hoping she would, though in my heart of hearts I didn't believe anything good would come of it. She wanted to see her granddaughter. I said, On one condition: you show me your family and I'll show you mine. She said she had another year until she retired and she couldn't do it until then. I didn't understand why the grave was dependent on her retirement. I flew over. I stayed with a friend. I asked Mom to meet. In a coffee shop.

I treated it as our last chance. I was tough, cold, and standoffish. I thought I was in the right. Mom's eyes were swollen, her makeup was smudged a little, and she had an elegant purse, her good luck charm. She brought it whenever she was meeting someone important and apparently it never failed her. We were sitting at a café table that held two cups of tea and a sugar bowl; above them, I locked my eyes on Mom and she couldn't withstand my gaze. I kept saying: contact with her granddaughter in exchange for the family grave. Tears ran down Mom's cheeks and finally messed up all her makeup. She begged me to wait a year. I didn't give an inch. A long silence fell. I had the feeling I was finally winning and Mom was giving in. She got up and went to the bathroom. She came back with her face washed and red. She put money for the tea on the table, took me by the hand, and we left. She told me to hail a cab. She got in and said: the corner of Anielewicz and Okopowa. The whole way, she didn't say a word, just cried. I didn't know where we were going. We held each other's hands but I didn't let her hug me. We got out of the taxi and in ten steps we found ourselves at the gate of the Jewish cemetery. Mom took a tissue out of her lucky purse and wiped her face thoroughly. Again, she took me by the hand and, looking every which way, grasped the handle on the metal gate.

We passed a little building and turned right. Mom was walking faster than usual, though every now and again she lost her way. After a few minutes, we found ourselves standing at something like an obelisk with a lot of different names on it. I asked what we were doing there. Mom said this was the grave I wanted to see so badly. But Mom, it doesn't have your maiden name on it. It's there, but it got changed when I was little. It expired.

I was finally standing at my grandparents' grave. Before it dawned on me that my mother was Jewish, I heard her say I was too. Mom, why did you want to wait until you retired to do this? Once you're retired then you're safe, my girl. They won't throw you out of your job, they won't take away your benefits. There's no more risk. Did Dad know? He didn't ask, and whenever I started talking about it myself, he'd wait for me to finish and never bring it up again.

After getting back to my new country I went to a rabbi to find out when my daughter's name day was. It turns out there's no such thing as a Jewish name day. I'm learning how to be a daughter all over again. My mom doesn't hiss anymore.

Bitter Chocolate

Somebody dies in every family—in ours, it was my mom. She wasn't sick for very long. I was too old not to remember her at all, but too young to be left with any specific memories.

All my sister and I had left was our dad and it was horribly sad for us. Still, we had school and friends, but he was alone. He was brave and kept soldiering on, and we did our best as son and daughter not to make things worse with our behavior.

With every year he grew sadder. He missed Mom badly, but he didn't talk to us about it. We didn't talk about her at all. A few years on, he fell into depression and stopped working; he almost didn't leave the house. He had a good pension, so I didn't worry about him so much. I figured meeting up once every few months was enough for us both. I have to admit this model of family life brought me a relief that at that time I couldn't do without.

When I was thirty, I went into therapy. Grief for my mom, a sad father, a sister I hadn't spoken to in years—I had some stuff to work out. The psychologist made me realize that in addition to all this heavy baggage I should add not having any grandparents. My mom's parents had turned away from my dad after she died. I never knew his parents.

The therapy had an effect. I started a family, I had a little son, I got in touch with my sister, and I started inviting my dad over for the holidays. At first, he wasn't up for it, but as the years went on, he started coming. He'd sit at the table and not say anything, but we were glad he was there.

He was part of the family landscape.

A couple of years ago he brought everyone bitter chocolate as a Christmas present. It was the strangest holiday of my life. He sat for a really long time without saying anything, but we were used to that. He was looking at my eight-year-old son and suddenly, when we'd finished the herring and were going on to the mushroom soup, he said to me, as though it were the most ordinary thing in the world:

"When you were the same age as he is, I wanted to kill you and your sister and commit suicide."

Before I could react, I heard my son ask:

"Daddy, why did Grandpa want to kill you?"

My wife took our kid into the other room and I stayed with my father, who was surprised by our response.

"Dad, why did you say that?"

"I remembered you were exactly his age back then."

"Why did you want to kill us?"

"Because I didn't want to live."

"But why us?"

"When I was your son's age, my mother killed herself. Before she did, she killed me."

"What do you mean killed you?"

"They revived me."

"Why did she do that?"

"She couldn't live alone."

"What do you mean alone? Weren't you there?"

"I wasn't enough for her. She couldn't stop thinking about her whole family, about how the last time she'd seen them was in the ghetto."

"In the ghetto? What were they doing there?"

"They were Jews there. Mama got me through the whole war but then she couldn't go on."

"You've never told us about this."

"And I'll never say anything about it again."

"You really wanted to kill us, Dad?"

"You think I'm joking?"

"I don't believe it. . . ."

"If Mama had succeeded, there'd be no more suffering in this family."

"I'm afraid you really think that."

"Soon you'll understand for yourself that suicide is hereditary."

My Five Jews

Pardon me, I'm not Jewish, but for years I've had a lot of trouble with you all.

When I was a little girl in elementary school, I'd already heard a lot about Jews. At first, I thought it had to do with smelling bad, since one of my friends wet himself once and it stank something awful. The kids called him a "smelly little Jew." Apart from that he was actually all right, but we still used to beat him up. I felt a little sorry for him, but I was ashamed to admit it. Sometimes we would walk home from school together, and once I even asked him why he was a Jew. He said he wasn't. That was my very first Jew.

I met the second at summer camp. He was short and wore glasses. At night, we'd all go and watch the Jew get burned. My friends would tie him to the bed, stuff scraps of paper between his toes, and light them on fire. He'd scream bloody murder and we'd shout that he'd be floating up through the chimney before long. A few days later his parents came and took him away. The counselors explained to them it was only juvenile game playing, that we were just kids, but they took him home.

The third Jew used to go to religion class with us, but right away we could tell something was wrong. We tied him to a pew in the church and said he had to tell the truth. When he admitted it, we let him go home. I never saw him again.

The fourth was a friend from my final year in high school. I was really disappointed in her, because I liked her, but she tricked me; she didn't say she was Jewish. I only found it out from other people after she'd left Poland. That just confirmed there's no trusting Jews. I had a friend in Israel and I met up with the girl there. I even invited her back to Poland, but she said she'd never come here because she had bad memories. What bad memories? She was the one hiding! It hurt me to hear that. She owed us so much and she ran away.

After that I tried to stay away from Jews.

When the new Poland came along, I mean before we managed to take our country back, they became our rulers. Suddenly they were everywhere: the whole government, the whole parliament. . . . Just everywhere.

A few years later I found out my friend from work was going out with a Jewish man. And he was my fifth Jew. I tried my hardest to discourage her; I did everything to convince her she was making a mistake. I said everyone would abandon her, she'd ruin her life, but it was no use; they got married. I didn't go to the wedding and neither did any of our mutual friends.

Just like I'd predicted, things started breaking down between us because of that Jew; at work we'd only say "hello" and that would be that. A few years later they left Poland. On the one hand, I feel really sorry for her, because she screwed up her life for that Jew, but on the other hand she got what she wanted. She could have had a normal boyfriend and stayed with her own kind.

I've seen a lot in my day. My parents passed away many years ago, my husband died young. My children are grown—I have more time to reflect. I guess a person has to have a personal brush with tragedy to get their brain and their heart moving.

How did we know that little boy who wet himself was a Jew? He had to put up with all that, even though he hadn't done anything. How did we know four-eyes at summer camp was a Jew? Maybe we were wrongly accusing him? How could we tie up that boy in the church? What was I thinking back then? And that Jewish friend, why was she hiding? After all, it wasn't her fault that she was born into a home like that. I started feeling really sad. Really sad. And then I remembered that friend from work too.

And maybe I'd been accusing innocent people?

I'd like to say sorry, but there's no one to say sorry to.

An Empty Jewish Soul

You get on a plane to Israel, your calendar is booked full with seeing people, but you've set aside some free time, because, after all, you know you'll meet someone and it's worth leaving space for them. You're on the plane, full of hope and open-hearted as usual, because it's not your first time flying.

You get off and hand yourself over to the immigration officer. You're full of understanding, you know that for our common good he has to be a little antagonistic, sometimes even aggressive. That's his job. You're sure he's a kind soul when he's off duty. Then you just grab your bag and walk confidently past the customs inspectors. You have to pretend to have absolutely no interest in them because (you think) that will guarantee they show no interest in you.

Finally, you're in Israel! Now you have to choose whether to run for the train or stop in the arrivals hall for a moment and watch the touching family reunions. I always stop and feast my eyes on their love. My favorites are the elderly people waiting for their children or grandchildren flying in. The elders cry and throw their arms around the youngest ones. They alternate between hugging and pulling away, as if they can't decide whether they'd rather feel them or see them. This ritual can be interrupted only by the middle generation. They also want to say hello, but now first and foremost they'd like to get to their destination, to their parents' home. I understand their hurry, but I could watch those tears for hours. Those are tears that, for a moment, liberate them from longing. They represent the happiest moment of their time together, since before long the countdown to parting will begin and that's not easy to be happy about, right?

I stand there for a bit and then head for the train. I could take a taxi but the train is more interesting. There are two groups of people on the platform. Group one—the ones who got here first, bought their tickets with no trouble, and are waiting patiently—are locals. After them comes group two— the diaspora and tourists. They look around nervously and are dressed too warmly. When you have to wait for a train that comes only every half an hour, it puts you in the mood to talk, to get to know one another and launch right into telling your family stories. The tourists don't play that game; they're worried about their hotels, the temperature, and their trips to Eilat.

This platform is the heart of the Jewish diaspora. Here, you are a Jew who's come to a Jewish country, but you can have some distance toward it. Here, an American Jew will talk to an Argentinian Jew about their crazy family they're going to spend the next two weeks with. They both laugh, but in the end, they say they'll have to think about retiring here. If you're a Polish Jew, you can also tell the story of your aunt who's already found a lovely girl who'll teach you Hebrew in no time flat. Your fellow passenger listens jealously. He got sent to a Jewish school when he was six and his Hebrew teacher wasn't a lovely girl at all.

You're happy, because on this platform you not only know you're part of the diaspora, you feel like part of it as well. It feels nice to belong to a community, you think. Finally. It was worth coming.

In the morning you walk to the shopping center to get some groceries. At the entrance, a woman is sitting on a wooden stool and playing a tune on the violin that seizes you right at the center of your Jewish soul. You stand there, listen, and wonder if maybe—someday?—you could live here too. An old man stands beside you with a horrible grimace on his face. Suddenly he goes up to the violinist and dresses her down in coarse Russian for not playing right. He takes the violin and shows her how she ought to do it. He looks at you for confirmation, but, after all, you're not a musician or even a music lover. Still, you feel really sorry for her, being humiliated in public like this. So, you tell him to give her the violin back, it was fine, we're not at the orchestra after all. The violinist looks at you gratefully and the guy hands her the violin back, gives you an unfriendly look, and tells her to repeat the last section. She repeats it, but it takes a few tries, and unfortunately not just two or even three, before he nods to say it was all right. He leaves her alone, shoots you a glance, and says: "Welcome to Israel! A country where everyone will give you good advice. Never leave your window open when you're having sex with your wife or anyone else. Before you know it, someone will decide to tell you what you're doing wrong and how you ought to do it instead. That's what our country's like. Now where are you from?"

You're right at the heart of well-being. You're among friendly people and slowly beginning to approach something resembling safety and a sense of belonging. You answer you're from Poland and immediately you regret stopping by the violinist. What attracted you? After all, she wasn't playing so amazingly beautifully. You could have listened to a couple of notes and gone to buy hummus and juice. But your empty Jewish soul let its guard down for a tiny moment.

This music teacher you've just met embarks on a violent, opinionated outburst about Jews who still live in the cemetery of Europe. Traitors to the nation, legitimizing Polish anti-Semitism by their presence.

Completely unexpectedly, you discover enormous strength within yourself. So enormous you could teach him to play the violin, maybe even give him some advice about sex. Your words, stated at higher volume than you'd intended, hearten the violinist most of all. You feel within yourself the strength of the last ones remaining, because if you can't defend yourself here, you won't be able to anywhere.

The Old Story

I used to drag one foot behind me, but if I could have, I'd have dragged both. I'd watch my mother's back getting further and further away and think I might finally wear through my shoe. I'd have been happiest if I'd managed to leave a permanent mark on the sidewalk. A sort of smooth trail as proof that we walked this way every day. Meaning Mom and I. Though we always left the house together, before very long I would be lagging behind.

Mom hated me for it. As we left the house, she would always look me dead in the eye in hopes that today I wouldn't drag my foot. She didn't say anything, her eyes just bored through my head like that. She'd help me put my shoes on, then my coat, then she'd look me in the eye, and then we'd set off.

By the age when I was walking to school, I'd already been dragging my foot for a long while. My shoe always wore through in the same spot and we'd have to buy a new pair, though only one was damaged, after all. The worn-through one always ended up in the trash, and Mom would put the second away on a storage shelf. They must have looked odd, sitting there by themselves. Single but together. If I'd dragged first one foot, then the other, it would have been less wasteful. That's what Mom said.

She was already very old. Or so I thought—all grown-ups seemed old to me when I was a little boy. Old and very tight-lipped. Though everyone apart from Mom watched with interest to see how far I got with my foot-dragging, Mom didn't look as I made my way along with my gaze fixed on her back; she never turned around. She'd walk and walk, then wait by the school until I'd shuffled the rest of the way. I'd pass her without even a glance. Now she was the one who had to look at my back.

I'd walk back from school normally. I went home by myself, so there was no need for dragging. I'd put one foot in front of the other, sometimes running, sometimes tiptoeing, and sometimes not giving any thought to how I'd walk. I just went home. There I also walked normally, even when Mom was right beside me.

Once I asked her when I'd started dragging my foot and she got horribly offended. Seriously and for a long time, maybe a whole month. I didn't ask again, but that didn't put my mind at rest. I'd examine my foot, looking for deformations or traces of surgery. It looked exactly the same as the other one.

*

When we were alone, Mom didn't speak to me. That is, she spoke a little, the way you do, about lunch and not forgetting my house keys. In the evening she'd check I was in bed and close the door to my room. On days when her friend Aunt Jadwiga came to visit—and she came a few times a week—Mom would also close the kitchen door. In there they'd talk, drinking cup after cup of tea, with Aunt Jadwiga smoking industrial quantities of cigarettes.

After Mom died, Aunt Jadwiga invited me to her house, which reeked of tobacco. There I was told that Mom loved me and she wanted Aunt Jadwiga to apologize on her behalf for being unkind to me on the way to preschool all those years ago.

And then the old story came back to me. We were on our way home on a rainy afternoon and to cheer Mom up I started fooling around. I jumped up and down, I made funny faces, but she was stoic as always. I started pretending I had a bad leg and I couldn't walk normally. Mom seized me by the hand and hauled me home. When I say hauled, I mean it literally. She pulled me along the ground, every now and then trying ineffectually to pick me up under the armpits. At home I got a spanking. And from that day on I dragged my foot. Mom and I had talked so little about it that I had almost forgotten how the whole thing had started.

I also remembered the one and only time in my childhood that I opened the door of my room in the evening. The awful stink of cigarettes wafted in from the hallway and I heard Mom say: "If his mama hadn't dragged that leg of hers, they'd have let her live. She wouldn't have gone to the gas."

Mom was really my grandmother, my mother was her daughter. There wasn't much that my mother-grandmother knew how to talk about apart from that.

The First Visit

Who knows best the paralyzing fear of the stairwell? A girl who's visiting her boyfriend's family for the first time.

I had no idea how it would go; he hadn't told me anything about them. I knew only that his sister, who I'd met a couple of times, would be there too.

We ring the intercom, we wait. Nothing. We ring again, wait, nothing. I give my boyfriend a surprised look. He's quiet, just like the intercom. What's going on? I ask. He says that we have to wait. I thought maybe they had a broken intercom. We stand there and wait. I'm very nervous and more and more weirded out. And suddenly, a miracle! The intercom buzzes, we can open the door. A little confused, but happy, I go up the stairs first. I hear a door opening above me. We get there, the door really is open, but there's no one waiting at it. I look questioningly at my boyfriend and he gestures for me to go into the narrow entrance room. Then he glances at my shoes, indicating that I should take them off. In our socks, we go up to the nearest door. A small room with a rug and a fully set table. We sit down and only then do I hear sounds from the kitchen. Of pots, not of talking. After a moment, a woman in a kitchen apron comes in. She's carrying a tureen of soup. She gently sets it down and greets me warmly.

Our hostess pours the soup. We're sitting at a table set for five, but there are only three of us. My boyfriend's mom tells him how her morning went and asks how we are. Suddenly she stops mid-sentence, smacks her forehead, and says, "I forgot to tell that dummy to come in for lunch!"

Fifteen years have passed since that visit. To this day I can't forget the sight of the disheveled man who walked into the room hanging his head. His wife didn't even glance at him and my boyfriend just gave him a quick look up and down. I got up to say hello. I offered my hand and he gave me his, weak and cold.

After the soup, the main course, and some apple cake with tea, we said good-bye and left my future parents-in-law, passing my brother's sister by the door.

In the car I peppered him with questions. What was that about? Why does your mom talk about your dad that way? Is he mute? Why didn't you say hello to him? He told me he's been that way forever. That it's a family secret, but he'd rather not talk about it. Well, I think to myself, what a fine mess you've gotten yourself into. You love a guy who finds something like this acceptable. You love a guy who doesn't respect his father and is afraid of his mother. Well, girl, you're going to have a great life with this family. Run away, I thought, get out, break up with him right away.

Today we have two children and a successful life. I went to visit my in-laws only another few times. My guy is a great husband, father, just a great person.

But after that awful lunch I decided not to let it slide and instead to find out what the hell was going on there. I thought up different scenarios. Maybe the father had killed someone? Or maybe he'd cheated on his wife? Was he mentally ill and they can't cope? My boyfriend didn't confirm any of my hypotheses.

Finally, I gave him an ultimatum: tell me what's going on or I'm out the door. And what does he say? That his father is Jewish. All right, I say, so what? And he tells me his mother doesn't respect his father because he was in the ghetto during the war. What difference does it make to your mother if he was in the ghetto? Was it some different ghetto than all the others? I shout. I guess it was the small ghetto, says my boyfriend, since Dad was small back then. Oh no you don't, I think, don't give me that! I'm not asking about how big it was, I'm asking about what your mother's deal is! After that we talked it over for many months, and it doesn't even matter how that conversation played out: we managed to stay together. We understand and accept one another.

I talk to my mother-in-law even less. Now she's changed and she loves her husband. It turns out his family owned half the buildings on the main street in our town. They've already recovered some of them.

My father-in-law still has sad eyes and walks around in old clothes, and I don't know how to explain all this to his grandkids.

The German Boy

The worst smell in the world came from a summer camp bathroom in the seventies. That combination of stinking crap, musty towels, and Pollena toothpaste.

I was eight years old when I went to one of those camps for the first time. Dad packed me a cardboard suitcase and, as a finishing touch, glued to the inside a page from my Polish class notebook with a bulleted list of every item in my wardrobe. How many pairs of socks, underwear, shirts, pants, sweaters, sandals, and tennis shoes, plus a towel, a pair of pajamas, and a toothbrush. As I packed to come home, I was supposed to check if I had every item on the list. Mom made me something to eat for the road. She wrapped my favorite roast chicken in paper and put it in a plastic bag. I also had some tea in a Chinese thermos that always gave my drink a chemical smell.

Thus equipped, in the morning they put me on a bus, a bulbous, light-blue Jelcz, full of unfamiliar kids. The counselor sat me with her daughter, who, before a minute was up, told me she'd never like me. Our bus was pulling a trailer full of older kids. The lucky ones sitting in the very back could look at the older kids and give us minute-by-minute updates of the faces they were making at us. Especially the oldest girl, who had big breasts. At rest stops we could get a closer look at them but they didn't talk to us.

We had barely set off when everyone started getting out their food. How weird, everyone had the same thing—kielbasa sandwiches, an egg, and a bottle of tea. In a second the bus was filled with all these smells mixed together. I felt a little nauseous, and a little hungry, but I could tell I'd look like an idiot with that chicken, so I didn't open my bag. The thermos was a dud too. Instead of listening to my dad and making sure it stayed upright, I put it under my seat. After a few potholes the thin silver filler cracked and the liquid spilled out on the floor. The counselor offered me some of her tea, but—wanting to come out with my honor intact—I said I never ate or drank while I was traveling, that it wasn't good for me.

We arrived in the late afternoon. We stood out on the field until they split us up into groups and cabins. The counselor read out my name and I raised my hand, took my heavy suitcase, and joined my group. The kids asked why I had such a weird last name, but before I could think of an answer, one boy said it must be German. I said yes and so I became the German boy.

I ended up having a very German evening and night. I

learned firsthand what we did to them. The kids weren't aggressive, but they were the victors. Meanwhile I was the one who'd lost the war. Since in my short life I'd already experienced being the Jew who killed Jesus, I thought maybe I was better off being a defeated German.

The bed was very uncomfortable. Instead of a mattress it had three pallets arranged crossways. It sagged horribly, this mattress they'd cobbled together, and made it impossible to lie on your stomach, which was the only way I knew how to sleep. Lying there awake, I could smell my mom's chicken, which I'd hidden under the bunk.

In the morning we were in that bathroom I mentioned at the beginning. We had new towels, so it only stank of crap and mint toothpaste. I was really looking forward to breakfast, since instead of dinner we'd just gotten sweet tea from a large urn. Unfortunately, breakfast was an unpleasant surprise: a bowl of cold milk and noodles. I'd never seen such a meal. I really didn't want to eat it, so I passed the time fishing out the milk skins and laying them along the edge of the bowl. The counselor said whoever didn't eat the soup wouldn't get bread and butter. And then that older girl with the big breasts appeared, the one from the trailer. She was just bringing up her own empty bowl. She looked at me, then at my soup, and asked if I was going to eat it. I shook my head. She took my bowl without a word and, a moment later, brought me back some buttered bread.

Our arrangement lasted the whole of summer camp. Even better, I became her favorite German. She taught me to smoke cigarettes, showed me where to buy sweet milk in a tube and how to blast a cigarillo out of its plastic mouthpiece at the shooting gallery. She held my head when I threw up after my first puff of tobacco and made me try again, because "it's only bad the first time." At the dance parties at night, she made the other boys jealous by dancing with me, even though I was only as tall as those breasts of hers. At the end of camp, she helped me throw away my mom's chicken, which had started sprouting maggots under the bed.

I grew to like the stinking bathroom, the breakfasts, the cigarettes, and my new friend, who also had a German last name.

Procession

Pilgrimage isn't the right word. Journey doesn't work either. Maybe funeral procession? That sort of fits and sort of doesn't, because a procession is full of people and I don't see anyone else around.

This procession of mine set off as soon as I asked my mom about her parents. I was a nosy little girl, but until that moment I could ask her about anything. On that day, when I broached the subject of my grandparents for the first time, my march began. That was the day I started to break down. My mind and my heart were breaking down, though I didn't know it yet.

I quickly accepted the conditions of silence. Maybe once or twice I tried asking again, but I didn't learn anything new. Instead of four grandparents I had two. My other two remained concealed beneath a thick blanket of wordlessness. Not a sound escaped from under it. I stayed silent too—until my two living grandparents died. Once I had no one of that generation left, I went on the attack. I asked my dad, I asked my mom—nothing. I begged, I threatened—nothing. I secretly rifled through the cabinets in their room—nothing. Then something strange happened to me. The family secret isolated me, condemned me to loneliness.

I understood I had to look somewhere else. I grew closer to databases and government archives than I was to my family home. It was by combing through them that I found my grandparents. Now I knew where they lived, what their names were, and how many children they had. I knew that in July 1942 they were arrested by the French police and taken, along with over ten thousand Parisian Jews, to the Vélodrome d'Hiver. The French state railroad transported them right to the doors of the gas chambers.

Yet beyond that I couldn't understand why my parents had put so much energy into keeping this information from me. Why in all the Jewish families I knew the dead lived on in the memories of their loved ones, but my grandparents had been exiled to the archives. Forbidden from reminding anyone of their existence.

I kept on the lookout for an excuse to talk, but I knew that I had to seize a moment when they wouldn't be able to ignore me or get away from me.

Then the ideal opportunity came along—my mother's uncle's birthday. My great-uncle remembers his sister, my grandmother, very well. They were very close siblings and he practically doted on all three of his nieces and nephews.

I waited through the aperitif, I waited through the appetizers, I even waited through the main course. Between the salad and the cheese course, I attacked. I tapped my knife on a wineglass. Everyone went quiet. They all probably thought I'd finally found a future husband. I launched my offensive and I have no regrets.

What about Grandpa? I ask. Silence. I know I've only got a moment, because before long my deep-laid plan will get that muffling blanket thrown over it and I won't be able to lift even one corner. I stand and shout that they have no right to cut me out of knowing about my grandfather. And who answers me? My mother, who gave me nothing but silence on this subject for thirty-five years. She screams that she's ashamed of me, that I've poisoned so much of her life, that she can't go on with this. She shouts that my grandfather was a coward, because if he'd listened to my great-uncle sitting here, he'd probably have survived. He and his family. But my grandfather knew best and didn't believe that he had to hide and wait it out. My coward grandfather believed in his French compatriots, who sent him and his whole family straight to the ovens in Poland. Almost his whole family, because she—my mother—was lucky to be staying with her aunt and uncle at the time. That's the kind of hero he was. He didn't want to listen to smarter people, and when the time came, he didn't even try to escape.

Now I barely speak to my mother. A little to my dad, but

he doesn't know how to fit in between us. My great-uncle is happy to be in touch, except I can't listen to his words of hatred and disdain for my grandfather.

My procession is still on its way. I've come from Paris by train, because that's how my grandfather and his family were brought here. I'm going to take the train all the way to Auschwitz.

Though mourners' marches end at the cemetery, mine is going to continue on, just in the opposite direction. I'm going to bring honor back to my grandfather. In spite of my whole family. And that's why I need you. You're the child of survivors, a psychologist and a photographer—no one will understand me better. I want you to make a portrait of me, but one that will let me connect with my grandfather. I've found documents in the camp archive. The Germans were methodical, doing their bookkeeping untroubled by guilt. My grandfather was murdered on September 20 at 6:05 p.m. They wrote that he died of a heart attack—the same as everyone else.

On September 20 let's meet at your studio and at 6:05 exactly you'll push the shutter release.

"Funeral procession" isn't such a bad phrase after all. All this time my family has been walking in it together, in silence.

Last Resort

I'm sorry to be so direct, but I need to ask. Do you know a lot about Jews? I hope that's not offensive.

I'm coming to you for help. I live in Łódź and I have a pretty nice life. I've got a successful wife, she gave me two sons; they're both almost grown up now. My brother and I run a pretty prosperous business. But you know how it is in Poland: if you do even slightly well for yourself you must be a Jew. At first, I laughed it off, because where do you even start?

My brother and I work hard and the results are plain to see. It seems like my boys might take over the family business. Luckily, they've both turned out to be hard workers. My brother has a daughter who's not interested, but the boys are champing at the bit.

Still, people talk. They congratulate us on our business and give us a wink. Two years ago, my brother couldn't hold back and socked one smart-ass in the mouth for calling us both Jews. It only got worse. Our employees talk about us behind our backs. They used to say, "Watch out, here comes the old man," and now it's "Here comes the Jew." We called in the division heads and started explaining who our parents were and where they came from. My niece made a family tree. We were surprised ourselves, because she came across a couple of coats of arms. We were even proud. But Poland is Poland; people had their minds made up. After all that, it got even worse.

We had one tough year and didn't give any bonuses, so what happened? Graffiti appeared, of Stars of David hanging from gallows. We were mad as hell because we'd been fighting hard for our people; we didn't lay anybody off, even though there were no bonuses. The cleaners didn't want to scrub off the graffiti. We had to clean it up ourselves at night.

Can you tell me what's wrong with these people? We're decent guys, we pay honest rates, with contracts, benefits, the works, and what do we get? "Jews, Jews, Jews!" We've had enough.

My brother and I have started trying to figure out, calmly, you know, what the deal is with this. We're successful so maybe they want to make our lives miserable out of jealousy? But that doesn't make a lick of sense. If our business goes under, they'll go with us. Don't they see that? Or if they get us really pissed off, we'll look for new employees. But where will that get us? "The Jews are even worse than they were before." It's all more than we can deal with.

You know a lot about Jews; what advice do you have? We can't let people get away with this. Do you know the effect it has on our families? My brother's in-laws already disapprove of him. His wife is pretty much sticking by him, but recently stuff between them is going downhill. It's understandable—she doesn't want to be a Jew. She thinks she's still got a choice, but I mean, even if she left him now, the damage to her is done.

You know, I wonder if it's because of how we look? My brother and I are dark, we haven't got your typical Polish bulbous noses, and our hair is curly and thick. If we didn't have this company people would call us "Gypsies." But we're Jews instead and I'm telling you it's a real pain in the neck.

People prefer doing business with their own, not with outsiders. But we're finding it easier to sign contracts with Germans than here at home. Now you tell me, isn't that proof we aren't the Jews people say we are? It's not like Jews are going to do business with the Krauts. . . .

I hope I haven't offended you; I mean, you understand this better than anybody.

Two months ago, my brother and I went to your religious community at our home in Łódź. We made an appointment with the rabbi there. At first, he was nice, he listened, he didn't interrupt. A few times he asked what this was about and whether we knew where we were. I don't know why he didn't want to help. We were asking politely. We were even prepared to pay good money. We understood it was an unusual question so we'd budgeted a suitable amount. But no dice. He wasn't willing to give us a certification.

You're our last resort. Please tell us who could give us some kind of certification. Or maybe you could write us something along these lines—that you hereby certify that the so-and-so brothers are not Jews?

Klementyna

A message on an answering machine: my name is Klementyna, but that's a pseudonym, just for the purposes of our meeting. I'm eighty-nine years old and I would really like to meet with you. Maybe you'll be tempted by the fact that I live in Łódź, or that I'm still hiding here. I hope you understand that I'm hiding not because I robbed a bank, but for a totally different reason. If you don't want to get on a train and come, I understand. But maybe you'll be intrigued by an old woman and her story that she's never told anyone before. Please think it over. To encourage you I'll add that this will be our first and last meeting. I'll be waiting.

What are you looking at me like that for? I'm old but I try to keep up a decent appearance. I'm ninety, but I tell everyone I'm eighty-nine, that sounds much better, doesn't it? Listen: eighty-nine. And now: ninety. There's a difference, right? Anyway, you wouldn't understand. Not now, though you will later. But I'll be gone by then so I won't get to say I told you so.

I dressed for going out—after all, I've got an appointment with a gentleman from Warsaw. Take a look: reasonably fresh loafers, a skirt as good as new, a blouse I haven't worn in twenty years, and a neckerchief that used to belong to my husband. You're waiting politely for me to start my story, and here I am yammering away because I'm afraid to begin. Do you know why I dragged you here? I had to tell someone that it's 2016 and I'm still hiding. It's been well over seventy years now. I can't believe it myself.

In 1939 I was living with my parents, because my older sister had been married for two years and had a young son. In 1940 they handed me over to some Poles to hide me and they all went to the ghetto. So that we don't have to return to the subject, I'll tell you straight off that none of them survived. I lived with a childless couple who got our apartment from my father in exchange for looking after me until the war was over. The husband was a little older than the wife, and they didn't talk to one another much. I won't give their names. They fed me and gave me a place to sleep. They kept their agreement with my dad. I survived.

The day after Łódź was liberated I walked out of that house and never went back. I didn't nominate them for a Righteous Among the Nations medal, nor did I thank them in any other way.

As soon as I started living with them I slept in the husband's bed. Not because I liked to. His wife slept in another room with the door locked. I think that suited her; she had peace. At first I thought this was how it had to be and it was the additional price for looking after me. Then I didn't think about it at all; my mind switched off completely. Between early May 1940 and January 20, 1945, I left the house three times. Each time the husband was taking me to a woman who gave me an abortion.

Right after the war, I found myself a good Polish boy with no family and we got married. I'd been looking for someone like him because what use did I have for some mother-in-law or sister-in-law nosing around, asking questions. No, I didn't tell him anything either. He died sixteen years ago and to the very last he never had an inkling of what I really am.

I don't know if you find that simple to understand or hard. Those were different times. We couldn't sit down at some fancy café on Piotrkowska Street, like the two of us are now, and talk about life.

I went to sleep beside my husband but I spent the whole night long in my mother's embrace. Sounds odd, doesn't it? At night I would play with my nephew, then in the morning I'd make my husband breakfast.

Do you know what I was doing? I was hiding, even though

the war was over. I was hiding my murdered family, who were already so well concealed that even I couldn't find them. I was deceiving my husband. I was deceiving my children. I was deceiving my friends and co-workers. I was deceiving the whole world! And you know why? So that I could live. Not so I could live better. I was doing it only so I could live! I was hiding from myself and I almost succeeded. Sadly, I decided to meet you and now it's all gone to hell. Don't worry, it's not your fault.

You get older and your mind starts to dwell on things. As soon as that starts, there's no going back. The train set off down the tracks . . . and took my world to the gas, but I didn't go with it. Many survived to tell their stories, but I survived to not whisper a word for all these years.

I gave birth to two daughters who don't know they're Jewish. They've got clear consciences now, because they're not deceiving their husbands. Both of them had daughters. I have Jewish granddaughters who will have Jewish children and will never learn the truth.

Nothing but girls. Clearly someone upstairs is battling with me.

I had to meet with you because you might prove useful as a mitigating circumstance.

Invisible Thoughts

My dad didn't love my mom, because he loved another woman. You didn't have to be Sherlock Holmes to see it.

It's really painful for children to be born into a household like that. I'm the oldest, I have two younger brothers. All of us could see it, but each our own way. I identified most with my suffering mom.

How does a child know her dad doesn't love her mom? An alert daughter can just tell. She'll catch one hostile glance, then another. A bitter smile or an unanswered question. I think a woman sees it faster than a man, and definitely faster than a boy. I saw it very early. Too early. I was angry at Dad. I'd spend more time with Mom; I wanted to punish him. I'd make a show of walking right past him, but snuggling up to her.

I loved them both, but I hated him too. That hatred boiled over and spilled out onto Mom. I was mad at her for letting him treat her that way, for not fighting for her dignity. Finally I turned my back on her. I spent many years vacillating between them.

How does a daughter know her dad loves another woman? It's not so simple, but daughters can be ruthless and they're capable of digging up things that their parents think they've done a great job of concealing. Dad sits there in an armchair in his own house and thinks we can't tell he's sick of us. And his daughter watches carefully. A moment of carelessness and she knows. Or doesn't know it so much as senses it. And if she senses it, she starts searching. Such a daughter is like a dog on the hunt: she'll follow a scent until she finds what she's looking for.

Even as a teenager I used to investigate him. I'd play hooky to find out who he was going to see. I had no luck; nothing suspicious ever happened.

My brothers didn't want to talk to me about it, though they kept their distance from my father. I guess they were trying to show that they didn't accept him. A few times I provoked my mom, but all I got from her was tears and I wanted details. Since that was how she was going to be, I turned back to my dad.

I became a daddy's girl. An attentive young woman who wouldn't disappoint him. Going with Dad to the movies, going with Dad to the museum, going on vacation with Dad, and on top of it, without Mom or my brothers. I couldn't see it then, but my actions hurt Mom. Maybe even more than Dad had.

I don't know if my dad deserved those few years of having

the best daughter in the world. Meanwhile I was actually an undercover spy.

After years of subterfuge, Dad started talking about the past. When he talked about his student hiking trips, he seemed twenty years younger. I could sense I was on the right track. College trips, friends, girlfriends. All the while I was careful not to spook my prey. I was tightening the noose.

It finally worked. I tightened the noose around my own neck. I squeezed the story out of dad: Mom looks a lot like the other woman. She had disappeared without saying good-bye and Dad ended up with Mom, who looked similar. She had the same eyes, nose, and mouth too. My mom even moved like the woman who ran away.

That woman lives in Israel, she has a husband she doesn't love, and, like my father, she has three children. I went to meet her because I wanted to know everything. We talked; it was even nice.

Her parents were afraid to stay in Poland after the war. They couldn't stand hearing remarks like, So, some of you got through alive after all? One day they told their twenty-three-year-old daughter that they were all leaving and she wasn't allowed to tell anyone. She couldn't even say a word to her beloved. She told me what their last moments together were like. My father proposed and she couldn't turn him down because she loved him very much. Nor could she reveal the truth, because she'd sworn to her parents.

I don't know if her children can tell that she doesn't love their dad.

My mom loved Dad very much, which is why she did her best to take the place of the woman he'd lost. All her life, until she found out I'd discovered their secret. Then her life was over.

Imaginary Friends

I'd rather tell this to a therapist, but I thought you deserve something out of life too. Do you like dreams? The kind you listen to, not see in your sleep.

Mine are unforgettable. Not because they're so beautiful or colorful. They don't strengthen your faith in the world, but they make for good stories. They start like fairy tales, like those sweet moments right before you doze off. They end like the dread right after you awaken.

Please don't be afraid; I'm not going to shock you with cruelties. Just ordinary stories.

They left on a train and didn't come back.

We arrived, but there was no one waiting for us.

I'm the last person on earth and I can't believe it.

My children are dead and I don't know what to do now.

I can hear them somewhere far off, but I keep walking and not getting any closer. I'm a childless mother; all I have left are voices to listen to.

*

I know my dreams, we're friends. People have different kinds of friends; mine are difficult but very close. They come by uninvited. They need a little bit of darkness, a bed, and some quiet. They're like lovers, but they don't bring fulfillment. Loyal friends never abandon you, so looks like they'll stick with me to the end of my days. They're really a drag—they spoil my mood—but without them life would be even harder.

I'll let you in on a secret. I sometimes have waking dreams. They appear as embryos of thoughts, and if I don't snap out of them in time, they can grow so wild that I lose control over them. They hurtle to an inevitable conclusion that robs me of my strength and my desire to live. They shatter everything else. My family life, my professional life, my relationships with human friends. Human friends are different from imaginary ones because they're not suited to the dark, or to quiet, or to bed. They're more demanding, which shows the advantage of the imaginary ones, who are always by your side. Who bring pain, though a very familiar one.

It's possible to live this way. It's even possible not to want to live any other way.

There can also be traitorous dreams. Ones that pretend to be different or new.

I'm waiting for a plane, now I'm in the last waiting room. All that's between me and boarding is a jet bridge. I look at the people around me—they're my companions for the next few hours. I'd love to strike up a conversation with someone. I catch the eye of some children; I make silly faces at them and smile at their parents. We listen to one announcement after another about our departure being delayed. Now I'm starting to make friends. They're the ones who don't look away. They're even willing to exchange a few words about our shared fate. Finally, the loudspeakers inform us that the fault has been repaired and we can board. We head onto the plane. We're a completely integrated group, we get along well. We walk full of hope. We sit down, buckle our seat belts, the plane starts taxiing and finally takes off. We eat our tiny portions with plastic utensils, we drink from mini-bottles. We're reaching cruising altitude, says the captain. And then everything starts to shake, the oxygen masks fall. Some people scream, others are paralyzed, children wail. And I, you see, I sit there and watch this as though I were from a different story. I observe from the sidelines and then I rise and start trying to cheer them up. The flight attendant shouts that I need to return to my seat, but I can see she's panicking herself. I know that in a few moments we'll be smashed to pieces on the beautiful mountains I can see out the little round window. I head for the phone the crew uses to make announcements. I pick up the receiver, push the button, and say: Don't be afraid, it won't hurt. Let's enjoy our last few moments. Just think, there have been people who went through weeks and months of fear, humiliation, pain, and hunger before they died. We're going to die today, but we've been free. Please, don't be upset, there's no reason to. Someone takes the phone away from me, so I return to my seat. I'm alone among many. I wait. I'm in my place.

I wake up very sad, because I saw myself waiting patiently for death.

Chess

I'm a secret Jew, you couldn't have invented a more curious specimen. I'll give you my life for a book. We'll make piles of money together, believe you me. You think I trekked this way on a train for nothing? A contract in two copies, date, signatures, bank details, and we're set for life. Please think it over. Meanwhile I'll tell you a few things from my life, to pique your curiosity.

I often fly to Israel, always on pilgrimages. No one has a clue that anything's up. I join groups from different cities and keep to myself, which under the circumstances is understandable. The whole time I stay a little apart. Maybe they think this guy is really focused, maybe he's suffering—they don't know. And since I don't encourage people to talk to me, we don't travel together, more like side by side. Once we've arrived, it's the same route as always. I'm telling you, I could lead people down the Via Dolorosa with my eyes closed. I know where the guide's going to make comments like: Well, unfortunately these filthy people have put their souvenir stands everywhere. I'm sorry you have to see this. They're not capable of respecting our faith.

When it's getting close to time to go home, I say good-bye to the group. I tell our priest guide that I'm joining a pilgrimage to Nazareth—which is true. Then I go to see my family in Tel Aviv. My mother's uncle used to live there, but he's passed away now. His children and grandchildren are my closest family. We spend a nice week together before I head for the place where Jesus grew up. We don't make a fuss about saying good-bye, because I'll be back in a year. We're long past talking about what my life is like and why I go through all this rigamarole. No, I won't move to Israel; I'm grateful for all the offers, but no. We've reached a family consensus. I want to live in Poland, so it's better I don't reveal myself, it's fine how it is.

After visiting a string of holy sites once again, as a very focused and unsociable pilgrim, I return to Poland. No neighbor or anyone I know catches me—I leave with a pilgrimage and I come back with a pilgrimage. I've got it worked out pretty good, you've got to admit.

Once I'm back I return to my normal life. Here, I'm neither a Catholic Pole nor a Jew. I pretend I'm grounded in reality, but I live without purpose. I have two lives. My everyday one is hard, but I know how to live it. Not reacting to an anti-Semitic article, not getting into discussions about Israel. Go to work, have a beer with people, and chat noncommittally.

Check if my salary came through, pay my rent, and await my swiftly approaching retirement. Easy-peasy. My second life is harder, because I lead it on my own. I think of my mom, who was so afraid that she didn't know how to tell me I had an uncle in Israel. I try not to think too hard about how I'm doing the same thing. In my second life for myself alone, I'm a Jew, but that begins and ends with the word "Jew." Three letters without any meaning filled in. As if I'd put them in random order and made the first one uppercase. I read, I watch movies, but I can't ask anyone about anything because my two lives don't mix. When I start feeling my second life is becoming emptier than my first, I push those thoughts away. I avoid closely examining my contorted lives.

I'm sure you're wondering why I wanted to meet in a hospital. No, I'm not sick or visiting anyone here. This is the hospital where my mother died. In the internal medicine department, she told me to swear I'd never tell anybody I was Jewish. She said otherwise she wouldn't be able to die in peace. You might think if I hadn't promised, she'd be alive to this day. I did what she wanted, I swore, and she did what she promised—she died.

Today's the day that I solemnly break that promise. A person can't live like this—without his own life. I have to be

Jewish with someone, at least for a moment. I can't keep sitting on my own listening to "Hava Nagila" and all that, which I don't understand anyway, though it still makes me cry.

Forget the contracts and the signatures. I thought I knew how to laugh all this off but I misjudged.

I'd like to know what you think of the Israeli-Palestinian conflict, about mixed marriages, about monuments to the Righteous, the Polin Museum, Judaism . . . about what that religion says about suicide, about a thousand other things that I've already talked about many times to myself, but without learning anything interesting.

I'm a Pole with a Jew living inside him, and a Jew who doesn't exist without that Pole. Now and then I play chess with myself and you know who wins? Sometimes one, sometimes the other.

The End of Time

You've got to race over this fragile ice as fast as your legs will carry you, because we all know how it's going to end. Best to float a tiny bit above the surface, to reduce the risk and extend your life. If your foot doesn't touch the surface it won't crack. And you fly along!

You know perfectly well there are no phoenixes anymore—they're passé—you know you've got only one chance.

You're a little girl—you've got a mommy. You get bigger—you start to understand you've got a daddy. You grow up a little more and now you know that Mom lives only for you. After a while it dawns on you that you too are only for Mom.

You know from her that time will suddenly stop. You don't know when, but it's certain knowledge. It will stop and it will hurt. But who will it hurt? What do you mean, who? You! It will hurt you! Because before you can get a look around, you'll be on your own.

You're aware of time, which is growing shorter. From the

very beginning you know the countdown has begun. You savor new connections, enjoy them, but you have to keep zipping along. You dump one partner after another. Not everyone understands it, but you haven't even got time to explain. You've got to keep running because only movement ensures existence. If you stop, you die—and you want to keep living, after all. You want to try everything because you've got only one life. And you know it will be too short.

You go back to Mom; you want to talk. You ask questions, make requests, you want to learn something. You don't ask about your father, you know that's not allowed. Asking about your grandparents is even more forbidden. Maybe about your childhood? About people the family knew? Their college friends? No! You won't learn anything!

You cut off contact with your mom and decide to take care of yourself. You go to a psychologist and every appointment throws you off balance. You're not going to spend money on that, you're not a masochist. You search for a more durable relationship, but you can't keep it up, you keep zipping along so life doesn't slip away from you and so you don't have to hear the thin ice creaking under your feet. You try once or twice again; finally you know you have to go back to Mom. You didn't succeed, but in a way, you did—the two of you are together again.

I look at Mom—she's up there in years now, she putters

around the house, she goes out less and less. She doesn't have to, she's got me. She drifts around the apartment and hums to herself. She never used to sing anything, but now she keeps murmuring something under her breath. When I finally ask what song that is, she says, What song? So, I start singing the tune to her myself. Mom looks at me and goes white, her eyes start brimming with tears. Each one pauses for a moment on the edge of her eyelid, as if wondering which direction to flow, then cautiously slips down between her eyelashes. The tear makes a second stop at the corner of her mouth, then it falls to her chin and drip-drips onto her blouse. I wonder, is this that cracking ice? Have I just reached the end of time? Whose end is it? Mom's or mine?

Mom doesn't say anything. The tears keep flowing and soaking into the fabric of her blouse.

I started looking for that tune. An app that recognizes music tells me it's a lullaby, with the lyrics written by Itzik Manger. Sad and beautiful, it's about winter and flying, but really about love and parting.

Mom died a few weeks later. After her death, in her house I found a piece of paper in her handwriting. The title read: "LULLABY," then everything was crossed out and only one part was legible:

The distant train will never come back,

                                      She was there,

Though the girl waits for it by the track,

                                      I was not,

She stands with grown-ups' legs all around

                              You aren't going to live this way,

Wearing her invisible crown.

At Hitler's

I went to Hitler's on vacation. I had a room with such thick walls that to open the windows you had to crawl into the recess. I didn't open them often because it was freezing cold. Even so I liked sitting on the sill and watching the snowflakes flutter down. These days the snowflakes aren't so big anymore; evidently all the big ones fell back then and now only the little ones are left. Or maybe I was smaller and they seemed larger? They've stuck in my memory because I watched them so closely, I couldn't believe each one was different. Even now I can't believe it.

We found Hitler's very hospitable. I was staying in a room with two other boys. One wore nothing but green and had unmarried parents, and the second wore glasses and was very afraid of the former landlord. When it was really cold, we stayed inside, then when the cold lifted, we'd go on expeditions. There was a lady looking after us who was on the older side. Now I think she wasn't even fifty. She made sure we cleaned our plates and checked if we had underwear on

under our pants. Apart from that we had a free hand. The
lady would also show up when we had dances with the girls.
She watched us dance but didn't intervene.

My friend with the green clothes and the unmarried parents didn't have an easy time with us; we teased him brutally.
To this day I'm ashamed of it. My friend who was afraid of
Hitler was calm only when he knew the exact schedule for the
day. What scared him most was lying in bed in the evening.
He couldn't take his eyes off the door and we kept asking
him if he could hear the sound of Hitler's boots striking the
floor. I feel awful about it now, but when we were young, we
couldn't hold ourselves back. The moment we started talking
about those echoing footsteps, he'd sit bolt upright in bed,
face white and ears pricked.

We often talked about the war. Green kid, with the unmarried parents, had family that fought somewhere in the east.
He didn't know where exactly, but he was proud of them.
Hitler kid's family also fought, but in some different war, because it was in Spain and France. He was proud of them too;
he even knew how to say a few words in French.

After the first week we forgave green kid for having unmarried parents. At the end of the day, we didn't care and
neither did he. Hitler kid wasn't so lucky. After a few days
he refused to leave the building. He said he liked it inside.
What had put him off was when we went to visit the win-
dowless structures they had there. Our guide really knew

his stuff. He kept saying, "Hitler used to walk out this way," "Hitler drove up on this road," "Most often Hitler stayed in here." The boy in the glasses walked at the back of the group, and when we stopped, he hid behind us and kept looking this way and that. Since he was the smallest, on several occasions the lady looking after us thought we'd lost him.

At the end of our stay, we learned we were joining the girls for a trip to the nearby town. We were happy because by then we were a little bored at Hitler's. Unfortunately, our friend in the glasses had to stay behind; he had a high fever. After we got back, we told him about the town and ice skating with the girls on a frozen pond. He asked us to bring him something to eat. It turned out he hadn't eaten since morning because he was worried that he'd run into Hitler.

After dinner we organized an illicit get-together with the girls. It was one of our most enjoyable evenings. All three of us did our best to be charming, and the girls behaved like ladies. We secretly ate cake we'd snuck in from the dining room. We drank tap water. We felt like grown-ups, sitting on our beds and talking seriously with the girls, who that night were grown-ups too.

By the next day we were preparing to leave. Packing, cleaning, looking for missing clothes, saying good-bye. Hitler kid didn't budge from his room. Only in the evening, when our counselor insisted, did he come to our closing meeting. The three of us went together, with him in the middle. We were sitting like that in the meeting when he said next year, unfortunately, he wouldn't be able to come. We went back to our room in identical formation.

That little boy in glasses who was terrified of Hitler was you. This happened in the mid-seventies, at a winter camp in the Masurian forest, set up in Hitler's former headquarters, known as the Wolf's Lair.

With Mom

What can a grown man talk about with his mom?

I could talk about anything. I'd come to her tiny, very noisy apartment, I'd sit in one armchair, she in the other, and we'd talk. There was a coffee table between us, and on it, a porcelain bowl with sesame-seed pretzel sticks, a silver non-heirloom sugar bowl, and the books Mom was reading at the moment.

She always sat facing the window, which made her eyes catch the light and the skin on her face look smoother. There was also a sofa we never sat on. It was always buried in newspapers and books waiting for their turn to be read.

That living room of Mom's was beautiful, warm, and promising. Family photos hung on the walls, but they showed only her descendants. There, in that living room, she had mothered dozens of Warsaw's survivors. People she knew who had decided not to leave the country in '68 and whose parents had passed away.

It's natural for an adult son to always ask his solitary

mother if he can help with anything—bring her something, sort something out for her. And of course I did too. Sometimes I'd even get tasked with something that made me feel needed. But that wasn't the essence of our times together.

I'd arrive with my mind full of questions. You see, I had a bit of a plan. I never got to carry it out, though, because Mom's very first answer sent the conversation veering off in such an interesting direction that there was no point sticking to it. Mom's inner restraints had been in excellent working order until Martial Law was brought in. On December 13, 1981, the dam burst and that very day Mom started telling me the story of what she'd been through during the war.

Now I could ask about anything.

I'd come, sit in the chair with my back to the window, and listen. We had our work cut out for us, because I found the stories that she told impossible to imagine. I listened and did my absolute best. Mom did too, but her story opened up a chasm between us. We were reaching the limits of shared language, a semantic void.

She told me that in the ghetto during the war she'd adopted a mouse and fed it with bread crumbs, which many people wanted for themselves. She told me that people in the ghetto needed love, because when the world's at its worst, a person wants to feel close to another person, to feel their warmth. She told me people could make love for hours, or even entire days, to avoid thinking about what was going on outside their bed. As I listened to her stories, I didn't think that love like that could produce children. Mom said the women in the ghetto stopped having their periods. The life cycle ground to a halt; nature didn't want to give them more lives for death to prey on. Right after the war people were looking for someone to start a family with, not necessarily to love. They got married and had kids. Maybe I too, like many children of my generation, had parents who didn't love one another.

Some are lucky, they can talk to their moms about family, romance, even about the Holocaust. That's nothing to sneeze at, because when you grow up in a post-Holocaust household, you can sense that your home is strange somehow and you'd like to know why.

Others are unlucky, because they were born to mothers whose lives began in '45. They keep doing the math but can never figure how their mom came into the world right at that moment. They search for photos, some trace of family, and find nothing. And now they never will find anything because when their mothers die, they take their sorrows with them in their entirety. Their family histories will get no life after death.

*

The mom I'm telling you about has two daughters, who are friends of mine. She isn't my mom. I chose her for myself and she embraced me.

I ended up with a mother who, after the war, lived a life she'd invented for herself. I've got many questions that now I'd finally know how to ask.

The Convent

There's nothing to like about the halls of a convent. Walking through them in solitude could only appeal to literary types. The old floors, worn down by many generations of feet moving like clockwork on the same route every day, stimulate writers' minds. Sitting at their desks, they hear the echoing steps of an old nun. Sometimes an uncertain novice will scamper around on the pages they've written, not yet worthy of a proper, reverberating footstep. The light forms gorgeous patterns on the walls, which have seen much in their time.

Do I surprise you? Please don't think you've come across a madwoman. Let me continue my story.

Strange that those who haven't lived in convents grant them tremendous respect, while those who've spent their whole lives in them bite their tongues.

✳

Convents are for those who want to be in them. Not for people who get sent there so they don't trouble the outside world.
Such people can't just leave, they have to wait for the world to
change, which can take a long while. Locked up among people
of faith, they themselves live without hope.

I can see you'd like me to tell a more concrete story, but please
believe me—it's just around the corner.

My mother found shelter in a convent. She was kept there and
that allowed her to survive the war. She transformed from a
Jew into a non-Jew, she eluded pursuit. A man her father knew
brought her to the gates. She was eleven and never saw her
family again. To her, the convent meant rescue and loneliness
in a single very poisonous combination. To enjoy life while
missing what you've lost is a task beyond the abilities of a
child.

More interesting now, eh?

✳

Mom left the convent as a Roman Catholic. I can't say through and through, though I'd like to say, no less than that Church's founder. She was fifteen, she'd been ready to take her vows and serve God to the end of her days, but the nuns wouldn't accept a Jew remaining there. There was no one waiting for her outside the gates.

She went to her family home, but a new family was living there now. She wandered. She turned down the emissaries from Palestine who wanted to take her to the State of Israel, which was just then being born. She met a man who remembered her parents. She married him in a Catholic ceremony—she was a Catholic, after all. For many years they had no children. That is, Mom didn't, because Dad had a son whose existence I learned about only once I was an adult.

Now I'll tell you about myself, since that's why I'm meeting with you.

I was born in 1954. At that time, we were living a few doors down from where my mom's parents had lived. Until 1968 I knew nothing about them. The word "Jew" was never spoken once in our home. When one of our neighbors said to my mother, "Get the hell out of here, you rotten kike, go to Israel," I froze with fear but also amazement.

At home we held a brief huddle. The idea that won out was one that to this day I can't understand. Dad thought of it and Mom agreed. I was sent to a convent, because "when bad times are coming, we hide Jews behind walls." In a single day I'd become Jewish and a faithful Catholic. That's how I came to spend almost five years in the company of a crucified Jew.

Permit me to sum up my story.

I thank the convent for sheltering my mother during the war. I hate the convent for what I went through there. I didn't speak to my father for the rest of his life and I'm trying to understand my mother to this day. Once I realized that there are countries where being Jewish isn't the only point of reference, I left Poland. I didn't want my children to end up in a convent.

Common Good

Where are the Jews of days gone by,
They went up the chimneys into the sky.

I've heard you quote that graffiti before, you know. But how should we understand it? Are the Poles somehow to blame for the fact that it didn't get painted over for so many years? Or maybe the fault lies in writing something like that at all? Now, I like you a lot, I go to your book events, but you're getting a little ahead of yourself here. Why make a fuss? So somebody wrote that. If it's hurtful, then roll up your sleeves and paint over it yourself. If it's still there, that must mean it's not hurtful. Anybody normal stopped noticing it long ago.

Why go on and on about it? And you're surprised people get testy when you do?

I haven't come here to be mad; I've come to help. You know why? Because I'm worried about you, you see? You're causing yourself problems, and it's just not worth it. You tell such beautiful stories about the Jews. Please don't stop, to us that's worth its weight in gold. But you've got to know when enough's enough, for goodness' sake! You want to convince the nation that the Jews were Poles. What for? Everyone's got their minds made up, meaning you've got to tell them little by little so you don't offend anybody. It's got to feel like it fits right, or else it'll chafe. But you go around stirring stuff up, if you'll pardon the expression.

Please keep painting a beautiful picture of that forgotten Jewish world for us, because we miss it. Talk about those people who lived in our beautiful country, our neighbors. You can bet everybody would love to hear something about them. But you can't forget to take responsibility for your own words, can you? You can't slander the nation, because this is the nation's home.

I worry, because when you people tell these exaggerated stories and it provokes a reaction, you immediately turn it into a scandal. You don't know how to sit quiet. And you're even more surprised to find yourselves alone on the battlefield. You see, when you start hurling accusations, don't be surprised if we don't join in. You understand that, don't you?

Who do you all owe your lives to? To us, the Poles, of course. We put our own families' lives on the line to save you, I'm sure you remember, don't you? But all we ever hear from your bunch is how the Poles were worse than the Germans. If you people want to keep living here, you'd better accept reality.

I hope you understand, I've got nothing against you. I'm simply trying to explain so that you can see the other side, or else there's no way we can understand one another. Please try to see from another perspective. For our common good.

I'm a history teacher and I always try to give my students an objective view of a situation. Regardless of the subject, I make sure historical truth is their guide. It's the same when it comes to the Jewish issue. I start at the very beginning, because context, you see, builds perspective. Well, who took the Jews in when no one else wanted you? The king of Poland, Casimir the Great—and thank goodness he did. How could he know what would happen here five hundred years later? Maybe he shouldn't have let you in back then, but never mind that. You arrived in our lands and, somehow, we worked it out, sometimes for worse, sometimes for better, but we managed to live.

People don't remember what happened hundreds of years ago, but they know well what happened during the war. Who helped the Russians kill our people? You did. Who ruled us after 1945? You did. Are you surprised that in '68 we cleansed our country? There was no other way; we had to fight so our people could rule themselves. That was the final moment—any longer and we'd have become an Israeli colony. That's the reality.

I'm sorry to keep rambling on and on. I hope I've helped you broaden your perspective. I can't wait to tell my friends that I opened your eyes to history. Do you mind? I'm looking forward to your next books. Don't forget that in a certain town you've got a fan.

Also, I've got a request, for an inscription. I bought this book for one of my students. She's very sensitive. Her name's Karolina, but I call her "my little black-haired girl." She cries so hard when she reads these things of yours, it's hard to describe. Maybe write for her: "To weeping Karolina, from the author." Please don't put a date, because I'm not sure yet when I'll give it to her.

Sweet Dreams

I don't remember much. I rested my head on her thighs, while my ears took in words about raspberry sorbets. Then I floated toward "the blue," as the poet wrote. A wonderful emotion. When a person has a flash of such rapture, he doesn't think this is a moment he has to preserve in his memory because it might never come again. He could listen to these little rhymes forever.

Things get complicated when you grow up a little. Mom likes to read, but mainly to herself. When I get up in the morning to walk to school, Mom hands me breakfast with the newspaper in her hand. I come home, she's reading a book. I eat lunch, she's reading something again. I talk to her and she looks at me, maybe she even smiles a bit, but she's somehow not very present. In time I get used to it. Well, maybe not to everything. The stink of her cigarettes really gets under my skin. When I get up in the night to go to the bathroom, I see Mom bent over a book with her glass of wine, amid clouds of smoke.

I'm big now, ten years old. I know Mom lived through the war. I know her parents, brothers, and sisters were killed.

I know she got the number on her arm from the Germans. None of this is a surprise; after all, I've always known. I'm used to her crying when she tells me about it. Mom doesn't talk to me about anything else, but I like to listen to these stories because I like her voice. Now and then she reads me a poem by Julian Tuwim.

> Denny lay on the grass,
> Looking up in daydream
> At the blue:
> "How sad the clouds floating past
> Aren't made of vanilla cream . . .
> Those pink ones far away
> Aren't raspberry sorbet . . .
> And these here, gold and flaky
> Aren't giant piles of pastry . . .
> I wish the entire sky
> Were made of chocolate pie . . .
> The world would be so sweet!
> I'd laze without a care
> No worries anywhere
> And reach up in the air
> And eat . . . and eat . . . and eat . . ."

I really enjoy the moments we spend together. This is our habit: she reads, I listen. We could just as well do it the other way around; I'd read and she would listen. We could even for-get the book—after all, we both know the poem by heart.

I become a young man and start to understand that Mom barely sleeps at all. She just reads constantly. She's not picky, she'll read anything. She uses these books to hide from the world. I used to think she was hiding from me.

I get mad. I don't let her tell me about the war and I make fun of our little poem. I yell that I can't listen to another word about someone just lying in the grass and looking up at the sky. What does he see there, that daydreamer of yours, I holler. He's got to come down to earth; you can't just live on dreams! How can he yearn for clouds drifting through the sky? Mom looks at me in a way she never has before. Her eyes are beautiful. Amid the tears I know so well, there's a hint of joy, something barely visible. That was the most wonderful moment of my life—the beautiful way Mom looked at me. Without taking her eyes off me, she picks up the book, opens it to a random page, and recites from memory.

Denny lay on the grass,
Looking up in daydream
At the blue . . .

I've heard that poem I don't know how many times, but this time it sounds somehow different. Denny lies there and gazes at the clouds in the sky, but now they've changed. My sweet dreams have dissolved. Thick smoke from burning-hot chimneys has covered up the blue sky.

I won't know how to daydream anymore.

One spring my mother jumped out a window. On the sill she left a copy of *Poems for Children* by Julian Tuwim with an inscription: "From Mom."

On the Aryan Side

We were three little girls in the cellar.

At the time I was nine, Hela was the same, and her sister Danka was six. We spent a very long time in the dark down there. Luckily, we had a little food with us and a few essential items.

All this happened in the cellar of a mountain cottage in Zakopane. I remember it like it was yesterday. Stairs came down from the ground floor, on the landing there was a bathroom, then another few steps down and you came to two rooms. One with a tiny window, the other totally dark. That's where the coal was kept, and we three with it. It was winter when we were down there; we wrapped ourselves in blankets brought from upstairs and chewed over our sorry fate. Every now and then we sent Danka to sneak us something from the kitchen upstairs. She brought us all sorts of treasures, most often meat and sausage. To this day I don't know how to explain it, but that's what happened.

At this time, I was called Miriam and we pretended that hiding like this was a vacation.

We set up a life for ourselves in the cold basement.

We had a basin, so we could wash. We even managed to bring a little mirror down with us. That made the time go faster. We'd do our hair up in imaginative ways and then look ourselves over like real grown-up ladies.

There were moments when our play was interrupted by sounds coming through the wall. We knew who was making that noise—Germans. Quiet through the wall meant time for us to play, footsteps and voices meant mortal terror. We worked out a whole set of hand signals we used to replace words.

We were experiencing these moments of danger at the end of my pregnancy. Luckily, we had water and the basin. On the way down, we'd grabbed two cloth diapers. We knew what was needed for a baby.

The labor was very difficult, because I had to be quiet. We were unlucky, because at that very moment the Germans returned to the other side of the wall. If they found out about us, that would be the end, they would kill us all, including the baby. I covered its mouth so it wouldn't make a sound. We were incredibly afraid that once it was born, the infant would start to wail.

I gave birth to a healthy Baby Born doll, which luckily

didn't make much noise. Our life started seeming rosier, now that there were four of us. But we had a lot of trouble looking after a newborn. There was no stove for us to dry the wet diapers on, nor running water. We sometimes forgot about the Germans and ran upstairs to the bathroom. Conditions were forcing us into increasingly risky behavior.

Each of us secretly dreamed of an end to our torment. Maybe we were even ready to be exposed, just so this could all be over.

One afternoon we heard troubling sounds, only not through the wall, but from upstairs. We huddled in the darkest corner of the cellar and waited for what fate might bring. Suddenly the door to our room opened. The villain found the light switch and flicked it on. Our surprise passed quickly; we started trembling: "Look out, a German! Run! Save the baby!"

We stopped yelling and he stood there and stared at us in disbelief.

He saw his two daughters and their friend who'd come to visit with her mom for winter break. We had our hair done up in misshapen little chignons. We were wrapped in dirty blankets and behind us on a wash line were two drying diapers that looked like they'd been used to clean the cellar floor. On the coal heap lay a naked Baby Born doll.

He tried to figure out what we were doing, but to us he was an invader from an evil world. We couldn't talk to him. We only informed him that we were Jews who had found a safe hiding space in this cellar, but he had ruined everything and because of him we were in danger of being killed.

He was momentarily speechless. I don't think he'd expected his house would be a hideout on the Aryan side of the ghetto wall. Once he'd snapped out of it, he ordered us to clean up the mess. He couldn't see that he hadn't interrupted our game at all—he was actually completing our story. We'd been discovered and we were begging for our lives.

My friends' dad was an avowed anti-Semite and this situation really made him uncomfortable. Nonetheless, he suggested we play in the living room, but that was the last place where we could hide. We explained to him over and over again, but he wouldn't relent.

We spent the last days of winter break 2002–3 playing dress-up as ladies from the nineteenth century.

The Chair

Some Jews recently wanted to take our chair away. A chair's just a chair, it wasn't even that comfortable, but we won't hand it over.

Years ago, my grandpa showed me the bottom of the seat had a smudged stamp that said "Germany." As he put the chair back on its feet, he muttered to me. He didn't say anything, but a thread of understanding had been tied. I thought it was clearly a looted chair. My grandpa is built like a tank, so who knows, maybe he just stole the chair from the Germans. And maybe that's the reason nobody sat in it. It stood in the kitchen between the tall cabinet and the window, the protruding windowsill slightly blocking it off. It acted as a place to put freshly brought groceries. It was black and ugly; it didn't match the other furniture. As far as I can remember it was never given the honor of being brought to the dining room table.

It would have stood there peacefully if not for the letter Grandpa got one day from Haifa. Grandma took it from the mailman and placed it on the cabinet by the front door. Grandpa came home, inspected the envelope front and back, and set it down again. For the first week, Grandma teased him that some pretty little Jewish girl must have fallen in love with him. Grandpa was stubborn. He didn't comment, he didn't open the letter.

The letter lay there in plain sight for more than a month. Mom pressured Grandpa to open it, but he didn't reply; he'd just give me a wink. I'd wink too, though I had no idea what he meant.

In the end, Mom couldn't resist and opened the letter from Israel herself. To our amazement it was written in Polish.

Greetings,

We are the grandchildren of Menachem, of blessed memory, who found shelter in your home along with his two sisters from 1942 to 1945. His sisters were killed two days after leaving your house, which you probably do not know. Our grandfather told us a great deal about you. After leaving Poland in early 1946 he never returned there. We understand that his experiences from the time of the Shoah kept him from going back, but we would like very much to meet you.

If not for you, there would be no us!
Let's meet!

If you would like to come visit us, we will cover all the expenses.
Please just write saying how many tickets to buy, for when, and what
names.

We await your reply, dear Polish friends.

Menachem's Family

Grandpa listened to her read the whole thing, gave a dismissive wave of his hand, and went out to the yard. To every question he answered: "Ancient history."

Neither he nor anyone from our family went to Israel.

The Israelis came to us. One day we saw them by our fence. You could tell from a mile away that they weren't from around here. Menachem's son was standing with his wife and adult son and daughter in front of our house.

Grandma greeted them with tea and cake. We had a hard time communicating because only the father spoke a little Polish. He said he knew exactly where his father and aunts were hidden but he had to go outside the house to find the place. His father had told him many times how he walked there in the dark.

We went outside the cottage and the counting began. Seven steps from the threshold, and then left, to the door to the kitchen. Then four steps, turn right, and another four. Bend over and lift the trapdoor to the cellar. It worked like a charm; the trapdoor was in the right place. The Israeli father looked questioningly at my grandfather, and Grandpa nodded. Their whole family went into the cellar and closed the trapdoor. Silence fell. After a moment, Grandpa bent over and forcefully pulled up on the handle in the floor. They emerged in silence, terrified.

The Israeli father looked around the kitchen and his gaze fell on the German chair. "Is that the chair my father sat in every night, looking out to see if any strangers were coming?" To which my grandfather replied: "That's the chair I put over the trapdoor whenever the neighbors came over. I'd sit in it until they'd closed the gate behind them.

"I'd sit there and pray for them to get out of here already."

The Israelis wanted to take their grandfather's chair as a memento, but we couldn't give it to them because it belonged to our grandfather. They suggested paying us for it but Grandpa wouldn't hear of it.

Once they'd gone, he took the chair to the woodshed, chopped it into pieces, and said: "I'm sick of staring at it, and they'll find life easier without it too."

Birthright

I was fifteen and, just like every year, I went to visit Grandma Bronka for summer vacation. I was listening to thrash metal, had grown my hair out, and was dressing pretty shabbily.

Grandma Bronka got the idea she was going to send her grandson to summer camp. That didn't exactly put a smile on my face, but Grandma kept praising the place to the skies. I knew she wasn't trying to get rid of me; she wanted me to go and have a good time. I didn't completely get why, but I didn't give much of a damn about anything, so summer camp was fine too.

I arrived, they gave me a room; it was pretty all right. The counselors were three years older than me, tops, and seemed decent enough. We always had something to do, it wasn't boring, but something about it all felt weird. Here we'd be going to a Jewish cemetery, or here we'd have some big discussion about Israel. Not that I had anything against it—I was more of a hippie than an anti-Semite—but something was off. Finally, I worked up the courage; I went to one of the counselors and I said to him: Listen, when are we gonna quit messing around with this Jewish stuff? And he gives me a look and says, Probably never. Wait, I think, what's going on here? I've got nothing against Jews, but how much can a guy take, you know? And he tells me practically everybody here is Jewish and you don't end up here by accident. Dude, I think, do you know something I don't? I ask him what I'm doing here. If you're here that means your Jewish family sent you. My Jewish family? What family is that? If you want, we can call the community and ask who sent you here.

I knew who sent me without having to call any community of theirs. I went to every camper and asked if they were Jewish. The results of my survey came in loud and clear: I was at a Jewish summer camp, everyone around me was Jewish. I couldn't understand how the hell I'd ended up here too. I called Grandma Bronka. Do you know where you sent me? How could I not know, of course I do. Well, then maybe you'll explain to me what the deal is with these Jews?

Grandma Bronka explained everything to me over the phone. She told me why she hadn't said anything before and why she could now. She knew my parents would never go near the subject and she'd been waiting for an opportune moment. For myself, I don't know what I'd do in her place, but I'm grateful to her for taking matters into her own hands. You know what she was waiting for? She thought it was better to find out you were Jewish after middle school, because any earlier and things were tough. Kids are mean, they could destroy someone that young. But Grandma, I asked, can't they do that later on too? They can, but by then you've got no choice, you've got to stand up for yourself.

I stayed at the Jewish camp until the end. I made good friends there and the counselors were okay folks. I don't know how to say it, I became a Jew or I kept being a Jew, but I didn't have a problem with it. I'd worked my way into that world.

A few years later I went on Birthright, this trip that's supposed to encourage Jews to become Israelis. You know, I wasn't far off from giving Aliyah a try. They took us all over Israel and kept encouraging us, and I thought it all looked fantastic. Everything was going great until we discovered how dirt-cheap vodka was over there. Instead of going to a club unlike any I'd ever seen in Poland, me and my friend bought a liter of booze. We woke up the next day and the whole area was in mourning. A bomb had gone off in that club. That's when I started understanding where I was. So much for Aliyah.

So no to Aliyah, but yes to partying. Me and my friend skipped out of Birthright for a day. We went to Haifa, because his cousin, a chemical weapons scientist, had promised to take us to the testing ground. The three of us climbed up some tower and looked at the stars at night, drinking schnapps and smoking weed. We were in heaven; Israel was luring me in again. We went back to Tel Aviv hungover, but the rest of the group was in worse shape than us. They'd been at the

Dead Sea and were so bright red that they looked ready for
the burn clinic. Plus, we brought a bag of weed with us back
from Haifa too. What a mess! Let's just say that bag made it
into the papers in Poland.

The time in my life when I felt the most Jewish was when me
and some folks I knew were cleaning up the Jewish cemetery
in Częstochowa. And we got rocks thrown at us. I don't know
if the rocks came at a good or a bad time, but I think about
them a lot.

I can say I'm a Jew, but I'm also a musician, so for me Shab-
bat usually falls by the wayside.

Horizon

Have you ever laid down a bedspread smoothly on the first try? Not that I battle with my bedspread a hundred times whenever I make the bed; I'm just asking if you've ever just gone up to your bed and bang! It's smooth. Almost never for me. It usually gets bunched up in that one corner you can't reach without crawling onto the bed.

Or when a cork breaks on you, do you ever immediately think it's a metaphor for your life? I mean, I know I'm being over the top, but tell me, does that happen to you? And when those gears start turning in your head, when everything lines right up like a series of disasters, you soon realize you're being too hard on yourself. Isn't it strange how it's easier to keep going like that than to snap out of it?

Or when you're eating something delicious and suddenly you realize this is only good food; it doesn't mean you've got a good life. But why shouldn't it mean a good life? Given that life is supposedly made up of just such small, good things.

You puzzle it over for a while and realize that you've let yourself be tricked again. That feeling of bliss nags at you, it wants you to cast off your grief. It means well, but the two of you can't figure out how to work together. You do your best to get your life under control, but it turns out the only thing you can settle down with is your sadness. How to leave it behind seems like a mystery. You do know that it's driven by a grief that has settled like thick fog over many generations.

Are you jealous of other people's lives? Not for anything major like having a great family, smart kids, just for having a normal life, feeling good. You call a repairman and you hear him coming up the stairs whistling a merry tune. Have I ever whistled anything at all? Let alone something merry. I haven't got the slightest memory. He's just walking and he's happy, he's got music in him, meanwhile I'm some other species of human. Why are those notes willing to frolic through his head but not mine? Do you think maybe it's because I give up before I even get started? To me, everything seems bad from a distance so I don't bother getting a closer look. Do you think something might appear better close up than far away? I'll never find out.

I do my best to look at things positively. I stretch out in a beach chair on vacation and gaze into the distance. And you know what I see? A crooked horizon. Not undulating, just crooked. Not level, you understand? Is it possible for a horizon not to be horizontal? I look and see that verticals are vertical, but the horizon isn't how it should be. Nothing to be done. Let it be how it wants to be. I'll stay how I am too. Maybe my life can't remain level because of events in the past. In my world the horizon doesn't stay straight, do you understand?

I'm thirty-five and my life is unbearably lonely. I sometimes have happy moments with people who, like me, lead a life you wouldn't wish on anyone.

They're close to me; in their eyes I can see my own tears.

A Jewish Barter

I'd been an idiot. I'd agreed to go to Auschwitz with a visitor from Israel. He'd made the request through an acquaintance and I wasn't assertive enough. I normally say "no" before they even make it to the question mark, but this time my heart went soft. I thought: What's the point of him going all the way there on his own? What a fool I am! I don't even know why, but damn it, I said yes. As soon as I did, it turned out this Israeli was already waiting in a rented apartment, not even far from my house! Before I could ask when I was meant to go with him, my friend told me: Hang on, he'll be right over and you can make plans. Within two minutes I already regretted it. I knew this guy would be the type who sticks to you like glue. You can't tear them away without everything else coming off with them.

He arrived. He looked nice, tan and smiling, but I was so pissed off at myself that, nice or not, I was already sick of him. What, Jews the world over are meant to help one another out? Well fine, but I'd prefer some other way of helping than taking someone to Auschwitz. Luckily, he wasn't too young, because explaining anything to someone like that is a pain in the neck. They've already learned everything in school and if they ask questions it's just to test you. My Israeli was a little over sixty. Maybe it won't be so bad, I thought. We agreed to meet by my car three days later in the morning.

He arrived punctually, which is really saying something for a person from the Middle East. And he didn't have an Israeli flag to parade around Auschwitz with. I know because I asked specifically—I had no intention of escorting an Israeli pilgrim on a triumphant march through the blocks of the camp. I'd seen that many times before.

We had a pleasant journey there. Where are you from? What did your parents do? Are they still with us? Well, we won't live that long. Who do you vote for? Are your children Jewish? Just chitchat.

When we started seeing road signs for Oświęcim I had to explain that yes, that was its Polish name, but no, the signs were for the city, not the camp. When we did start seeing signs for the camp itself, my passenger went quiet. He looked out the window as if searching for something to help him understand what was going on here. I'd done the same on my first visit. He spotted some people and asked if those were Poles. Yes, those are Poles, my dear friend from Israel, but be careful not to confuse them with their grandparents or the grandparents of today's Germans. He listened; he didn't comment.

The parking lot. We get out of the car. By now the Israeli looks more wan than tan. We walk past the ticket counters; entry is free. We won't be taking a guide; I should be enough on my own. We walk through the gate that everyone recognizes, and then it starts: Tell me everything your grandparents told you. Everything? We haven't got time for all that, I want to make it home tonight for dinner with my wife.

I didn't even tell him half. He had so many questions that I couldn't keep up with my answers. Did they wash? How often? What about winter? Did they eat standing up or have somewhere to sit? How much time did they get for meals? Were they always getting hounded around or did they have moments of rest? What do you think, would the two of us have survived?

Enough, I say, enough! Stop asking questions, because no matter how many questions you ask, you won't understand. I know because I used to ask questions, then finally I gave up. It worked. He was struck dumb. After five minutes he was clinging to me like a wet old raincoat. I put him in the car, fastened our seat belts, and we drove home. My new friend had fallen in love with me. Evidently extreme experiences bring people together.

But what good is his pain to me? I've got plenty of my

own. We drove along quietly, night was falling, and suddenly he said he'd like to go with me to see the rest of the camps. Oh, come on, I think to myself. If you want to kill yourself, go ahead, but leave me out of it.

I lost. The two of us did the grand tour of the camps in Poland.

A few months later he invited me to lunch in Israel. His elderly mother, his wife, his children, and his neighbors were there. He seated me next to his mother so I could talk to her in Polish. I heard a lot about Poland and Poles. I didn't learn anything new. My friend's neighbor was very moved, because the Polish reminded him of his parents. He didn't say anything, he just kept nodding.

My Israeli friend decided to repay me for the time I'd spent on him in Poland. He took me to Masada. It was a sort of Jewish barter: I give you murder in the camps, you give me Jewish suicide. What are we doing here, I asked at Masada. Looking for strength and hope, he replied.

I went back home. I've stopped answering calls from my friend, I don't respond to his emails. For now, I've decided to live. I don't know how to find hope in Masada.

Bringing Families Together

Those who survived were divided into two groups: those with photos and those with nothing.

My dad was a photographer, which in the postwar world was a pretty great job. For the first few months his studio was located outdoors. He'd set up the camera, hang a curtain, sit his subject down, *click*, and it was done. Later he managed to occupy a basement whose beautiful wood floor was still intact. It's important for a photo to have a good floor. People preferred coming to Dad rather than to studios with chunks of rubble lying on the ground.

Dad took every kind of picture, from ID photos to family portraits that would get sent to relatives abroad to show who'd survived. There were wedding photos and portraits of the Soviet soldiers who took a liking to my dad's studio. We lived pretty well thanks to those Russians. They were steady customers. Dad spoke decent Russian and was capable of matching them drink for drink. Some photo sessions ended with Mom and me having to carry Dad home. The Russians got a driver to pick them up—he had it worse, because he had to lug them on his own.

There were also people who came not wanting Dad to take their pictures, but bringing treasures of their own. A piece of a photo, because the rest had burned. Torn prints, scratched and water-damaged negatives. Dad took pictures of these scorched photos and printed them so that the nonexistent part was restored. This wasn't some sorcery; he drew in the missing elements and did it so you wouldn't notice. He meticulously arranged torn pieces of photos next to one another, clicked the shutter, and created an image of this jigsaw puzzle. In the prints he retouched the connections and the picture would look as good as new. Damaged and dirty negatives would be put in a special bath. He'd make them into photos that were no worse than fresh ones.

Right after the war he was doing well, but the more time went on, the worse it got. All the local Russians already had several photos apiece and they got bored with drinking vodka with Dad. So, he started specializing in bringing families together. People would bring him a photo of a child, a photo of a mom, and a photo of a dad, and he would combine them so it looked like they were all standing together. Sometimes a mother and child would bring a prewar photo of a father who'd died. Dad would look the photo over, then set up the mother and child in front of the camera in a pose that matched the one in the old photo. I don't know how he did it, but it made his customers happy.

Dad said it wasn't so hard setting up the lighting so the living matched the dead. The problem was arranging the pictures so they didn't overlap. Normally, when people stand next to one another, someone is a little more in front and someone else is a little more behind. One covers the other up a little. And *that* was the biggest issue. They had to stand alongside one another, because when the living started pressing up against the dead, in the picture ghosts appeared.

Customers were prepared to pay even for unsuccessful photos. Once Dad spent a long time convincing a woman that he couldn't combine a picture of her husband and son, who had both passed away, with her own portrait so that everyone was in a tight embrace. She insisted and Dad finally acquiesced, and gave her a photograph where she had three eyes, because one of them was her kid's.

My parents' relationship was harmonious; there was only one thing they argued about. Mom begged Dad to leave Poland and he shouted that he never would. Yet leave we did. My father finally saw that a society ashamed of its actions would sooner or later turn against the witnesses of those actions. They didn't feel like waiting for a repeat of the Kielce Pogrom.

But he didn't feel at home in Israel. He said at his age you can't trade a familiar fear for new problems. After a few years, he died.

Mom and I cleaned out his studio. We sold the cameras and enlargers. We organized his archive, getting rid of the photos that had no value to us and leaving the ones of friends and family.

In there he had a collection of photos of our neighbor from Poland, but Mom didn't let me keep them. I also found many prints of the portrait of our family that always hung in my parents' room. The one where I'm dressed in a white play-suit and sandals—I can barely stand yet—and my parents are on either side, holding my hands. In the same envelope there were also three other photos: me with some people I didn't recognize and two portraits of my parents.

Only then did I realize the hands holding me up in our portrait didn't belong to Mom and Dad. Because theirs should have overlapped with mine, but these ones gripped me with a certain sleight of hand.

Anatevka

I research familial bonds between the living and the dead—
I'm a genealogist. I am the hope for a family reunion that may
bring relief, even just for a while. I've seen a lot of relief pass
too quickly to enjoy it, but still, I keep seeking opportunities
for even a momentary connection.

People phone ahead for an appointment or arrive without warning. They can be kind or unpleasant and demanding.
Uncompromising and hostile or open and cooperative. Different. As people are. As Jews are.

These ones here came without warning. An American
couple in tourist garb. They were both wearing these strange
pants that you could zip off in two places, turning them into
either Bermuda shorts or short shorts. Maybe they were going
straight from Warsaw to some lake, to wade around in the
reeds? They were also wearing very expensive hiking boots,
which didn't look very comfortable for walking around the
city. Their jackets suggested "new technologies so you never

sweat or freeze." And each with a little backpack covered in waterproof material.

They looked like they were on an expedition. Maybe that's just what this trip was for them. A journey into the unknown. Sadly, they were ill-prepared—they'd packed the wrong travel kit.

"We're here to find out something more about the town my father comes from," says the man. He opens his backpack and I wait expectantly for whatever he'll take out. Sometimes people bring such treasures it's hard to believe. Like documents someone sent to relatives abroad just before the war and which today are the only evidence that an entire town ever existed. Unfortunately, to my chagrin my visitor pulls out a large notebook and opens it to the first page, clean and unblemished. He's waiting for the first pieces of information.

I ask: "And what do you know about this town?"

"Not much, basically nothing. I know what it was called."

Well, that's something already! I grab a pencil, primed to write, and I can't believe my ears: "Anatevka." "Anatevka?" I ask. "Yes, why do you sound surprised? That's where my father grew up." Gosh, I think to myself, maybe the legendary shtetl was real? I only know it from *Tevye the Milkman*, but truth be told I'd never checked if anything like it existed. Maybe I was wrong? I start searching online. There is no such town. I search databases. There was no Anatevka. Or not in any of the sources I have access to, anyway. This is an awful turn of events. Here, sitting in front of me, is a descendant of a Polish Jew and all I have to say is his father couldn't have lived in Anatevka because it never existed. I'm a little apprehensive, but I say directly: "Sir, I've looked in every possible archive and nowhere can I find an Anatevka."

"You call yourself a professional and you can't find a town the whole world has heard of?" He looks at his wife, who shakes her head in disbelief and rolls her eyes. "Poland, I told you. We've got nothing to look for here."

I'm groping for life preservers. "Why don't you give me your dad's name and maybe that way we can track him down?"

It really is a Jewish name; it couldn't be more Jewish. Unluckily for me it's also very popular. Without violating client confidentiality, I can say it was like looking for a John Smith in the United States.

I enter it into a search engine that reaches the furthest depths of the surviving archives. I turn the screen around and my visitors and I start examining the fates of all these prewar John Smiths. After forty minutes they're running out of patience. We haven't even gotten halfway through and they won't last much longer, I can see with my own eyes. The woman is playing with her smartphone. The man gets up, but he doesn't leave; instead he takes off his jacket. That means he's determined; maybe he has faith in my knowledge and skills after all.

We start again from the beginning, though now there's only

two of us. The woman has gone to a café next door. I turn off the computer and ask how he knows that's where his father came from. He gives me a look of unfortunately anything but respect and starts to tell me the story:

"Many years ago, in the late seventies, my parents and I were watching *Fiddler on the Roof*. When the camera showed the town where it took place, Dad stood up and said: That's my shtetl, look, that's exactly where I grew up.

"So, who's right? You or my dad?"

A Joke for You

You've got no sense of humor. This stuff isn't that serious. I mean it is, but you don't have to talk about it that way. Why make people sad or, God forbid, frightened? You have to tell cheerful stories, but do it with a serious look on your face. You've got to tell them Jewish style, you understand? Other people laugh at their own jokes; that's not the right approach. You only tell a joke apropos of something, not just because you happen to remember one. If you remember one, good for you, you've got a great memory, but tell us something about something. Make it a riposte that stops the conversation in its tracks. When the laughter is followed by silence, that means everybody got it. The more they laugh, the longer the silence will last. Not that I'm in favor of huge silences, but sometimes they're a sign of reflection. You know that joke about two guys who run into one another for the first time in a long while? One says:

"I've missed you so much and I'd love to hear how you're doing, but darn it, I haven't even got a spare moment, so go on and tell me in one word how you're doing."

"Great."

"Goodness, I feel so unsatisfied. So many years and you tell me only one word. Of course, I know I'm the one who asked because I'm running late, but you know, I'd still like it if . . . I hope it's not too much trouble . . . could you tell me in two words how you're doing?"

"Not great."

There, you see, what a story. But there's no reason to worry about these two fellows anymore because they've either died or left the country. Or do you know the joke about the Jew who people keep asking to emigrate? I say asking but they're not asking, they're throwing him out on his ear. So, he sits himself down and wonders where to go. He thinks back on all the cities he's been to, the histories of different countries flash through his mind, but somehow, he can't choose. He asks the people who want to get rid of him to hand him a globe. He sets it on a table, spins it this way and that, frowns, ponders, spins it again, and finally says: "Have you maybe got a different globe?"

I'm sure they didn't crack a grin, but you would if you'd heard that for the first time, right?

Jokes have to be—how can I put this—they have to be

conclusive. Yes, conclusive. With a rhythm. First come curiosity and tension, then the punch line and laughter, and in the end, everyone gets left alone with their thoughts. And if not alone, then all the worse for them.

You know that joke about the guy who's getting rolled on a gurney down a long hospital hallway? They keep going and going, the lights on the ceiling keep flashing by, he's got one nurse in front and another behind. Nobody says a word, the trip is sort of dragging on, so this patient, out of curiosity but also out of ordinary politeness, tries to strike up a conversation with the nurses:

"Gentlemen, where are you taking me?"

"To the morgue."

"But gentlemen! I'm alive, aren't I?"

"We can see that, but we've still got a ways to go."

Funny, right? Could you tell the stories in your books in an upbeat way like that, give the sadness a little break? It'd take the heat off you and they'd get what they deserved.

The best jokes are about sex, health, and death—there's no escaping it. But the most dangerous ones are about politics, because sooner or later those will land you behind bars. You'd better leave those ones be; it could be hazardous for your health.

Oh, here's a joke. An old man goes to the doctor. The doctor asks him what he can do to help. And the man says he wants to piss normally, because now it keeps coming out just drip, drip, drip. The doctor asks:

"How old are you?"

"Ninety-five."

"Well then, you've done enough pissing already."

I think it's funny, but you don't totally get it yet. I hope you live long enough to. . . . Actually no, that's not a good thing to wish someone.

You know, to tell jokes well you've got to have some years under your belt. A young fellow won't do a good job, but an old man will. Well, unless you're too old and the joke just makes people feel sorry for you.

I've got a joke for you. An old man goes to a sperm bank and says he wants to donate his seed. The nurse at reception looks confused and asks how old he is. Ninety-three, shouts the old man, but age doesn't matter. If my wife came here, she'd tell you I've still got it. And do you know why she's not here? Because after what we got up to this morning, she hasn't got the energy to drag herself out of bed. The nurse apologizes to the old man, goes into the back, and hands him a plastic container. She shows him the door and says there are some men's magazines inside. I don't need any magazines, he shouts. After a while the nurse can hear the groaning behind the door getting louder and louder. The nurse knocks and asks if everything's all right. Sure, what wouldn't be all right? he says. I just can't get this damn jar open.

We have jokes because we haven't got any hope. But we sure know how to laugh, don't you think?

Stagnant Waters

How often I've wondered: should I talk to you, Mr. Grynberg, or not? We've known each other for so many years. I want to offer you a couple of reflections; you can even write them down as your own.

I'm afraid you won't be done working on the past by the time the future arrives. You don't write fast enough. Hurry up, because a sin of omission weighs heavily in the final reckoning.

You've already got the war settled. The postwar, in part, as well.

Maybe the time's come to look from a different perspective? Might you float up into the air a little and get a bird's-eye view? But you'd better give it some thought, because what you'll see can't be unseen. You'll be stuck with it for sure, and who knows if you'll be able to pass it on to others. One more risk.

I think you realize the place you live in is drying up. If you'd been born a few generations earlier, you'd be living right in the middle of a gushing current. You wouldn't even stop to think about it. And now where are you? The same geography, but the hydrology—the Jewish hydrology, you might say—is totally different.

Look closely. Can you see you're living in an oxbow lake? The river meandered this way and that, but your section broke away and lost its vigor. Do you see that? Or maybe you don't want to?

There are people in this world who think there are none of us left here. To them, there are so few of us it might as well be none. Let's not waste time wondering why they think that. Clearly, they have their reasons.

After all, we know that we're alive, that we're here.

Where is "here"? A place where there's nothing left even to reflect in the water's surface? There are no rivers, there's no current; all that's left are shrinking puddles and mud. Yes, Mr. Grynberg, you're too late, the river has flowed away. And don't you go thinking that as far as all this is concerned you're an assimilated Jew. You didn't choose that for yourself; it was the movement of the water in the natural environment that chose it for you.

Some people are born too early, but we were summoned here too late. In order to keep on living, we have to understand the consequences of that.

As consolation, I'll tell you there are also people who think you do exist. To them you're a curious case. So curious you're worth inviting over. They'll pay for your plane ticket and hotel accommodation. You're convenient, because thanks to you they don't have to come here themselves. You don't even have to dress up like a Jew from Poland; you can come in your own clothes.

What could be better, Mr. Grynberg—it's well worth putting in appearances all over the world, at no cost to yourself. Financial cost, I mean, because the other kind, well . . . you've never taken such an expensive trip in your life. Right away, from the very beginning, you can feel it. They need you to make themselves feel better. They give you the tiniest hint of that, as gentle as possible, almost imperceptible, but you're sensitive enough to tell. They let you feel they're better off because they don't live in an oxbow lake. Then little by little they'll loosen up, until one of them inadvertently, or seemingly inadvertently, just blurts out what he thinks of splashing around in that stagnant mud.

And what will you do? Give him a punch in the mouth for being an anti-Semite? Or maybe walk away? You won't punch him and you won't walk away because you're too polite. I'd punch him *and* walk away. There's no point listening to them, Mr. Grynberg. They're incurable. Even their parting words will be how sorry they are you have to go back. And you won't punch them in the mouth then either.

Think long and hard before you accept one of those

invitations. It's not worth it, because it hurts. It is worth it, because you grow wiser. The choice is yours. If you're wondering, I don't go anymore. On top of everything else, why put your own head on the chopping block? You don't look like a Hydra to me, so just forget it.

As far as good advice, Mr. Grynberg, that's all I've got. The issues of the next generation are beyond my jurisdiction now. What you'll give your children is your business. If you know how to pass on happiness to them, then congratulations, though when it comes to joyful inheritances, call me a skeptic.

And now you'd better catch up quick, because maybe this time fate will give you the chance to write stories in real time.

Unless you know how to outrun events and, cursing the past, write a happy ending.

Notes

Page 11: *It's 1968 and Jurek has become Jewish through and through.*

In 1968 the Polish communist government launched an "anti-Zionist" purge of Poles with Jewish backgrounds. Ultimately at least thirteen thousand were stripped of their citizenship and forced into exile.

Page 76: *At a winter camp . . . set up in Hitler's residence, known as the Wolf's Lair.*

The *Wolfsschanze*, or Wolf's Lair, was one of Adolf Hitler's headquarters during the Second World War, built in the forests of East Prussia. After the war, this region was taken over by Poland and the area became a popular tourist attraction. The Wolf's Lair is now a museum.

Page 92: *On the sill she left a copy of* Poems for Children *by Julian Tuwim.*

The Polish-Jewish poet Julian Tuwim (1894–1953) was one of Poland's most influential writers and his works, especially for children, remain popular to this day.

Page 115: *They didn't feel like waiting for a repeat of the Kielce Pogrom.*

On July 4, 1946, in the central Polish city of Kielce, forty-two Jews were killed and over forty were wounded by a mob of ethnic Poles. It sparked a large wave of Jewish emigration from postwar Poland.

Translator's Note

Mikołaj Grynberg's work is not so much polyphonic as clamorous. It's the sound of many voices pushing their way to the front, vying to be heard. This book's Polish title, *Rejwach*, is a Polish Yiddishism meaning just this sort of cacophony, a holy racket deeply rooted in Jewish culture and history.

The first time I met Mikołaj Grynberg, at a literary festival in Szczebrzeszyn, I was immediately drawn to his own voice—gentle, wise, and mordantly funny. But I was also struck by the voices he drew out: Grynberg was running workshops in oral history, teaching, as he has all over Poland, how to craft literary texts from one's own personal and family stories.

He teaches this because it's his own life's labor. Grynberg is best known in Poland for his works of documentary nonfiction, collecting the stories of his generation of Polish Jews—those born after the Holocaust and raised by survivors. Published in interview form, these books—most famously *Oskarżam Auschwitz* ("I Accuse Auschwitz")—bear witness to whole lives lived in the shadow of intergenerational trauma.

In *I'd Like to Say Sorry, but There's No One to Say Sorry To*, his first work of fiction, Grynberg seeks to tell these personal stories in literary form. He told me these stories began as fragments—"haikus"—that he built out. Their miniature form is a reflection of Grynberg's taste for the laconic, an acknowledgment that silence sometimes speaks as loudly as— or more loudly than—words. The clamor is perforated with gaps that stand in for experiences both inescapable and too painful to remember.

Though rooted in a catastrophic past, Grynberg's work is fundamentally about the present. At a time of mounting official anti-Semitism in Poland, when many inside and outside the country see no place in Poland for Jews, Grynberg's testimony of a Jewish present—a Jewish *presence*—is radical. I see in it echoes of the Yiddishist concept of *Doikayt*, "here-ness," which claims that the place where Jews belong is exactly where they are.

Indeed, Grynberg describes his own Polishness as deeply rooted. Its basis is the Polish language itself, a homeland of words. So how can a translator bring these words to a new homeland, one, as he puts it in "Stagnant Waters," with different geography and hydrology? I do not share Grynberg's gift for brevity, so my translation had to be pared down. His work was informed by generations of Polish-Jewish cultural and family memory. I, neither Polish nor Jewish, had to research, ask questions, check and double check and triple check. Grynberg vividly imagined each narrator in this book—I thought of friends, of family, and watched videos from the Yiddish Book Center's remarkable Wexler Oral History Project, to understand what these narrators might sound like if they were speaking in English.

I also turned to others for help. My tremendous thanks to Lauren Goldenberg, Arielle Angel, and *Jewish Currents*, who saw my early translations and published Grynberg in English for the first time. To Julie Enszer and The New Press, who recognized this book's importance and saw fit to bring it to readers in its entirety. To Jo Glanville, who has helped raise Grynberg's profile in the wider Anglophone world. To my mentor, Antonia Lloyd-Jones, for introducing me to Grynberg and agreeing to share the work she began with him. And finally, above all, to Mikołaj Grynberg himself, for his patient answers, his insight and wit, his beautiful writing, and his friendship.

How are we to understand the product of this collective effort—the translation you now hold in your hand? Mikołaj is a photographer, like my father. I have often thought translation and photography have much in common. Both are disciplines that walk the line between art and craft. I also believe both, in their own way, are documentary. I have tried hard to document, to bear witness to, Mikołaj's work. Like the relationship between a photograph and its subject, a translation is not so much a copy of an original text as a likeness. There are many metaphors for translation, and I hope this one unmasks some of the stinginess of the cliché "lost in translation." A photograph does not obscure its subject. Instead, it shows us something we might never have seen with our own eyes.

Sean Gasper Bye
Philadelphia, 2021

About the Author

Mikołaj Grynberg is a photographer, author, and trained psychologist. He has published three collections of "conversations" based on the oral histories of Polish Jews since the Holocaust: *Survivors of the 20th Century*, *I Accuse Auschwitz*, and *The Book of Exodus*. *I'd Like to Say Sorry, but There's No One to Say Sorry To* is his first work of fiction and his first work to be translated into English. It was a finalist for the Nike, Poland's top literary prize. He lives in Poland.

About the Translator

Sean Gasper Bye has translated work by some of Poland's leading writers, including Małgorzata Szejnert, Szczepan Twardoch, and Remigiusz Ryziński and is a winner of the EBRD Literary Prize. He lives in Philadelphia.

Publishing in the
Public Interest

Thank you for reading this book published by The New Press. The New Press is a nonprofit, public interest publisher. New Press books and authors play a crucial role in sparking conversations about the key political and social issues of our day.

We hope you enjoyed this book and that you will stay in touch with The New Press. Here are a few ways to stay up to date with our books, events, and the issues we cover:

- Sign up at www.thenewpress.com/subscribe to receive updates on New Press authors and issues and to be notified about local events
- Like us on Facebook: www.facebook.com/newpressbooks
- Follow us on Twitter: www.twitter.com/thenewpress
- Follow us on Instagram: www.instagram.com/thenewpress

Please consider buying New Press books for yourself; for friends and family; or to donate to schools, libraries, community centers, prison libraries, and other organizations involved with the issues our authors write about.

The New Press is a 501(c)(3) nonprofit organization. You can also support our work with a tax-deductible gift by visiting www.thenewpress.com/donate.

ALSO OF INTEREST FROM THE NEW PRESS

Black Moses: A Novel

Alain Mabanckou

The Death of Comrade President: A Novel

Alain Mabanckou

Eichmann's Executioner: A Novel

Astrid Dehe and Achim Engstler

Four Soldiers: A Novel

Hubert Mingarelli

ALSO OF INTEREST

ALSO OF INTEREST

Still Life: A Novel

Zoë Wicomb

Suncatcher: A Novel

Romesh Gunesekera

When We Were Arabs: A Jewish Family's Forgotten History

Massoud Hayoun

Wrestling with the Devil: A Prison Memoir

Ngũgĩ wa Thiong'o